THE
WILD
ROBOT

THE WILD ROBOT

WORDS AND PICTURES BY
PETER BROWN

Little, Brown and Company
New York · Boston

Little, Brown and Company

Hachette Book Group
1290 Avenue of the Americas, New York, NY 10104
Visit us at lb-kids.com

Little, Brown and Company is a division of Hachette Book Group, Inc.
The Little, Brown name and logo are trademarks of Hachette Book Group, Inc.

The publisher is not responsible for websites (or their content)
that are not owned by the publisher.

First Edition: April 2016

Library of Congress Cataloging-in-Publication Data
Names: Brown, Peter, 1979–
Title: The wild robot / by Peter Brown.
Description: First edition. | New York ; Boston : Little, Brown and Company, 2016. | Summary: Roz the
robot discovers that she is alone on a remote, wild island with no memory of where she is from or
why she is there, and her only hope of survival is to try to learn about her new environment from
the island's hostile inhabitants.
Identifiers: LCCN 2015021094| ISBN 9780316381994 (hardback) | ISBN 9780316382014 (ebook) |
ISBN 9780316382021 (library edition ebook)
Subjects: | CYAC: Robots—Fiction. | Survival—Fiction | Animals—Fiction. Friendship—Fiction. |
Islands—Fiction. | BISAC: JUVENILE FICTION / Animals / General. | JUVENILE FICTION /
Action & Adventure / Survival Stories. | JUVENILE FICTION / Animals / Bears. |
JUVENILE FICTION / Animals / Ducks, Geese, etc. | JUVENILE FICTION / Robots.
Classification: LCC PZ7.B81668 Wi 2016 | DDC [FIC]—dc23
LC record available at http://lccn.loc.gov/2015021094

20 19 18

LSC-C

Printed in the United States of America

To the robots of the future

ey
W
vl
pu

CHAPTER I

THE OCEAN

Our story begins on the ocean, with wind and rain and thunder and lightning and waves. A hurricane roared and raged through the night. And in the middle of the chaos, a cargo ship was sinking

down

down

down

to the ocean floor.

The ship left hundreds of crates floating on the surface. But as the hurricane thrashed and swirled and knocked them around, the crates also began sinking into the depths. One after another, they were swallowed up by the waves, until only five crates remained.

By morning the hurricane was gone. There were no clouds, no ships, no land in sight. There was only calm water and clear skies and those five crates lazily bobbing along an ocean current. Days passed. And then a smudge of green appeared on the horizon. As the crates drifted closer, the soft green shapes slowly sharpened into the hard edges of a wild, rocky island.

The first crate rode to shore on a tumbling, rumbling wave and then crashed against the rocks with such force that the whole thing burst apart.

Now, reader, what I haven't mentioned is that tightly packed inside each crate was a brand-new robot. The cargo ship had been transporting hundreds of them before it was swept up in the storm. Now only five robots were left. Actually, only four were left, because when that first crate crashed against the rocks, the robot inside shattered to pieces.

The same thing happened to the next crate. It crashed against the rocks, and robot parts flew everywhere. Then it happened to the next crate. And the next. Robot limbs and torsos were flung onto ledges. A robot head splashed into a tide pool. A robot foot skittered into the waves.

And then came the last crate. It followed the same path as the others, but instead of crashing against the rocks, it sloshed against the remains of the first four crates. Soon, more waves were heaving it up out of the water. It soared through the air, spinning and glistening until it slammed down onto a tall shelf of rock. The crate was cracked and crumpled, but the robot inside was safe.

CHAPTER 2
THE OTTERS

The island's northern shore had become something of a robot gravesite. Scattered across the rocks were the broken bodies of four dead robots. They sparkled in the early-morning light. And their sparkles caught the attention of some very curious creatures.

A gang of sea otters was romping through the shallows when one of them noticed the sparkling objects. The otters all froze. They raised their noses to the wind. But they smelled only the sea. So they cautiously crept over the rocks to take a closer look.

The gang slowly approached a robot torso. The biggest otter stuck out his paw, swatted the heavy thing, and quickly jumped back. But nothing happened. So they wriggled over to a robot hand. Another brave otter stuck out her paw and flipped the hand over. It made a lovely clinking sound on the rocks, and the otters squeaked with delight.

They spread out and played with robot arms and legs and feet. More hands were flipped. One of the otters discovered a robot head in a tide pool, and they all dove in and took turns rolling it along the bottom.

And then they spotted something else. Overlooking the gravesite was the one surviving crate. Its sides were scraped and dented, and a wide gash ran across its top. The otters scampered up the rocks and climbed onto the big box. Ten furry faces poked through the gash, eager to see what was inside. What they saw was another brand-new robot. But this robot was different from the others. It was still in one piece. And it was surrounded by spongy packing foam.

The otters reached through the gash and tore at the foam. It was so soft and squishy! They squeaked as they snatched at the fluffy stuff. Shreds of it floated away on the sea breeze. And in all the excitement, one of their paws accidentally slapped an important little button on the back of the robot's head.

Click.

It took a while for the otters to realize that something was happening inside the crate. But a moment later, they heard it. A low whirring sound. Everyone stopped and stared. And then the robot opened her eyes.

CHAPTER 3

THE ROBOT

The robot's computer brain booted up. Her programs began coming online. And then, still packed in her crate, she automatically started to speak.

"Hello, I am ROZZUM unit 7134, but you may call me Roz. While my robotic systems are activating, I will tell you about myself.

"Once fully activated, I will be able to move and communicate and learn. Simply give me a task and I will complete it. Over time, I will find better ways of completing my tasks. I will become a better robot. When I am not needed, I will stay out of the way and keep myself in good working order.

"Thank you for your time.

"I am now fully activated."

CHAPTER 4

THE ROBOT HATCHES

As you might know, robots don't really feel emotions. Not the way animals do. And yet, as she sat in her crumpled crate, Roz felt something like curiosity. She was curious about the warm ball of light shining down from above. So her computer brain went to work, and she identified the light. It was the sun.

The robot felt her body absorbing the sun's energy. With each passing minute she felt more awake. When her battery was good and full, Roz looked around and realized that she was packed inside a crate. She tried to move her arms, but they were restrained by cords. So she applied more force, the motors in her arms hummed a little louder, and the cords snapped. Then she lifted her hands and pulled apart the crate. Like a hatchling breaking from a shell, Roz climbed out into the world.

CHAPTER 5

THE ROBOT GRAVESITE

Those otters were now hiding behind a rock. Their round heads nervously poked up, and they watched as a sparkling monster emerged from the crate. The monster slowly turned her head as she scanned the coastline. Her head turned and turned, all the way around, and it didn't stop turning until she was looking right at the otters.

"Hello, otters, my name is Roz."

The robot's voice was simply too much for the skittish creatures. The biggest otter squeaked, and the whole gang suddenly took off. They galloped back across the robot gravesite, flopped into the ocean, and raced through the waves just as fast as they could.

Roz watched the otters go, but her eyes lingered on the sparkling objects that littered the shore. The objects looked strangely familiar. The robot swung her left leg forward, then her right, and just like that she was taking her very first steps. She stomped away from her crate and over the rocks and through the gravesite until she was standing above a broken robot body. She leaned in and noticed the word *ROZZUM* lightly etched on the torso. She noticed the same word on all the torsos, including her own.

Roz continued exploring the gravesite until a playful little ocean wave washed over the rocks. She automatically stepped away from it. Then a bigger wave sloshed toward her, and she stepped away again. And then a gigantic wave crashed over the rocks and engulfed the entire gravesite. Heavy water pounded against her body and knocked her to the ground, and her Damage Sensors flared for the first time. A moment later, the wave was gone, and Roz lay there, dripping and dented and surrounded by dead robots.

Roz could feel her Survival Instincts—the part of her computer brain that made her want to avoid danger and take care of herself so she could continue functioning properly. Her instincts were urging her to move away from the ocean. She carefully got to her feet and saw that high above the shore, the land was bursting with trees and grasses and flowers. It looked lush and safe up there. It looked like a much better place for our robot. She had just one problem. To get up there, she would have to climb the sea cliffs.

CHAPTER 6
THE CLIMB

Crack!
Thunk!
Clang!

Roz was having a little trouble climbing the cliffs. She had a new dent on her rear and a long scrape down her side. And she was just about to get another ding when a crab scuttled out from under a piece of driftwood.

The crab looked up and immediately showed off his giant claws. Everyone was afraid of his claws. But not the robot. She just looked down and introduced herself. "Hello, crab, my name is Roz."

After a brief standoff, the crab cautiously backed away. And that's when Roz noticed how easily he moved over the rocks. With his wide stance and his grippy feet, the crab could crawl up and down any rock face. So Roz decided to try out his climbing technique. She spread her arms wide and clamped each of her hands onto the cliffside. She jammed one foot into a crack and lifted her other foot onto a narrow ledge, and just like that she was climbing.

Roz moved awkwardly at first. A chunk of rock crumbled in her hand, and she had trouble finding footholds. But as she climbed higher and higher, she started to get the hang of it.

Seagulls squawked from their cliff nests and soared away when the robot came too close. But Roz paid them no mind. She was focused only on getting to the top. Up and up and up she went, methodically climbing past nests and ledges and tiny trees rooted in the cracks, and before long our robot felt the soft soil of the island beneath her feet.

CHAPTER 7

THE WILDERNESS

Animal sounds filled the forest. Chirps and wingbeats and rustlings in the underbrush. And then, from the sea cliffs, there came new sounds. Heavy, crunching footsteps. The forest animals fell silent, and from their hiding places they watched as a sparkling monster stomped past.

But the forest was not a comfortable place for Roz. Jagged rocks and fallen trees and tangled underbrush made it difficult for her to walk. She stumbled along, struggling to keep her balance, until her foot snagged and she toppled over like a piece of timber. It wasn't a bad fall. No dings, no dents, just dirt. But Roz was programmed to keep herself in good working order, and once she was back on her feet, she immediately began cleaning herself off. Her hands darted around her body, quickly brushing and picking off every speck of dirt.

Only when the robot was sparkling again did she continue through the forest.

Roz stumbled on until she found a patch of ground that was flat and open and carpeted with pine needles. It seemed like a safe place, and safety was all the robot really wanted, so she stood there, motionless, all perfect lines and angles set against the irregular shapes of the wilderness.

CHAPTER 8

THE PINECONES

If you stand in a forest long enough, eventually something will fall on you. And Roz had been standing in the forest long enough. A gentle wind whispered through the treetops, and then—*thunk!*—a pinecone bounced off her head. The robot looked down and watched the pinecone roll to a stop. It seemed harmless, so Roz went right back to doing nothing.

A few hours later, a gust of wind rushed through the treetops and then—*thunk!*—the robot looked down as another pinecone rolled away.

And then a few hours after that, a howling wind tore through the treetops. It bent trunks and shook branches and then—*thunk thunk thunk!*—pinecones began raining down. *Thunk thunk!* Roz felt something like annoyance. *Thunk!* She quickly scanned the area for somewhere safe from pinecones. And she spotted the perfect place when she looked up at the huge, rocky shape that towered above the forest.

CHAPTER 9

THE MOUNTAIN

Roz was now stomping her way up the mountain. Dense forest and rocky outcrops forced the robot to zig and zag and backtrack, but after an hour of steady hiking, she arrived at the craggy mountain peak.

Grasses and flowers and shrubs sprouted from every pocket of soil. But there were no trees at the top. Roz was safe from those annoying pinecones. She dusted herself off and then carefully climbed up a leaning slab of stone, to the very highest point of the entire mountain.

The robot slowly turned her head completely around. She saw the ocean stretching to the horizon in every direction. And in that moment, Roz learned what you and I have known since the beginning of this story. In that moment, Roz finally realized that she was on an island.

Roz looked down and surveyed the island. Starting

from the sandy southern point, the island grew wider and greener and hillier until it finally jutted up into the rocky cone of the mountain. In some places the mountain fell away, leaving sheer cliffs. A waterfall rushed off one cliff and fed a river that wound its way through a great meadow in the center of the island. The river flowed past wildflowers and ponds and boulders and then disappeared into the forest.

Blurry shapes suddenly cut through the robot's vision. She refocused her eyes and saw vultures circling above the foothills. Then she noticed lizards warming themselves on a distant rock. A badger peeked out from a berry bush. A moose waded through a stream. A flock of sparrows turned in perfect unison above the trees. The island was teeming with life. And now it had a new kind of life. A strange kind of life. Artificial life.

CHAPTER 10
THE REMINDER

I should remind you, reader, that Roz had no idea how she had come to be on that island. She didn't know that she'd been built in a factory and then stored in a warehouse before crossing the ocean on a cargo ship. She didn't know that a hurricane had sunk the ship and left her crate floating on the waves for days until it finally washed ashore. She didn't know that she'd been accidentally activated by those curious sea otters. As the robot looked out at the island, it never even occurred to her that she might not belong there. As far as Roz knew, she was home.

CHAPTER 11

THE ROBOT SLEEPS

Roz stood on the peak and watched the sun sink behind the ocean. She watched shadows slowly spread over the island and up the mountainside. She watched the stars come out, one by one, until the sky was filled with a million points of light. It was the first night of the robot's life.

She activated her headlights, and suddenly bright shafts of light were beaming out from her eyes and illuminating the whole mountaintop. Too bright. So she dimmed them. Then she turned them off and sat in darkness and listened to the chorus of nighttime chirps.

After a while, our robot's computer brain decided it was a good time to conserve energy. So she sat and anchored her hands to the rocks, her nonessential programs switched off, and then, in her own way, the robot slept.

CHAPTER 12

THE STORM

Roz felt safe up on the mountaintop. So she spent the next few days and nights perched on the peak. But everything changed one afternoon when a low-flying cloud crept up the mountain and Roz found herself surrounded by white. When the world faded back into view, she noticed more clouds floating south past the island. Then she heard a deep rumble behind her. The robot turned her head around and saw that the sky was filled with a swirling wall of darkness. Light flickered here and there. More deep rumbles.

A storm was approaching, and it wasn't just any storm. It was as fierce as the one that had sent the cargo ship to the ocean floor. The wind picked up, and the first drops of rain tapped against the robot. It was time to go. Roz unclamped her hands and began sliding down the peak.

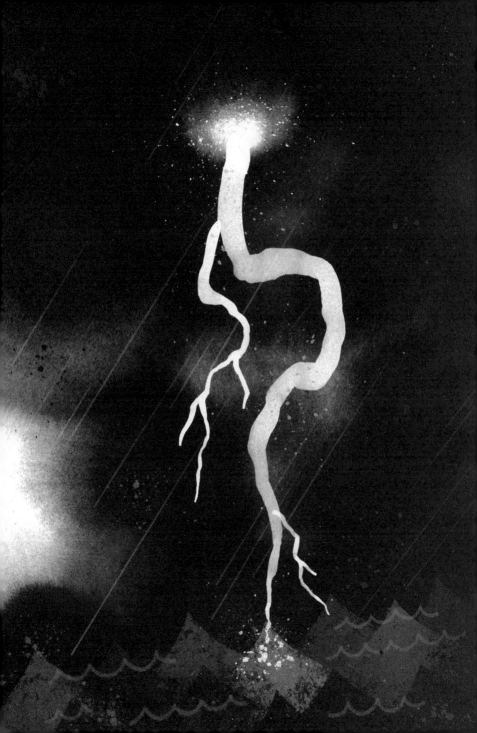

Hot sparks flew from where her body scraped against the leaning slab of stone. As soon as her feet hit soil, she was off and running.

The rain fell harder.

The wind blew faster.

The lightning flashed brighter.

The thunder cracked louder.

So much rainwater was falling that rushing rivers of runoff started springing up everywhere. Roz splashed down the mountain, searching through the gloom for any kind of shelter. But she should have watched where she was going. Her heavy feet slipped and tripped, and she tumbled right into a mudslide.

Our robot was helpless. The river of mud whisked her downhill, slamming her into rocks and dragging her through bushes and sweeping her straight toward a cliff! Mud was pouring off the cliff like a waterfall! Roz frantically clawed at the ground, grasping for anything she could hold on to, but the flow only carried her faster toward the edge. And just as she was about to plunge over the side, she came to a hard, sudden stop.

Mud surged around her, spraying into her face and pinning her against some solid thing. She blindly felt with her hands and recognized the thick roots and trunk of a pine tree. In an instant she was pulling herself up into the branches. The wind whipped across the mountainside and Roz heard the familiar *thunk!* of pinecones pelting her body. But she didn't mind them. She was just happy to be safe from the mudflow. The robot locked her arms and legs around the tree and waited for the storm to blow over.

CHAPTER 13

THE AFTERMATH

Daybreak, and the storm had passed, but the sounds of water were everywhere. The air was filled with the dripping sounds of mountain runoff and the sloshing sounds of flooded streams. And then came a very different sound. It was the clanging sound made when a robot slips on a wet rock. There were quite a few clangs that morning.

As Roz worked her way downhill, she scanned the aftermath of the storm. Giant mounds of mud and debris had formed below the cliffs. The island's central river had crested its banks and spilled into the nearby fields and forests. Some trees had been uprooted. Others were submerged, their upper branches barely poking above the floodwaters, their lower branches swarming with fish instead of birds.

After such a storm, you might expect to see animal

corpses scattered among all the devastation. But the animals seemed to have survived just fine. Somehow, they had known the storm was coming, and they had found shelter long before it rolled in. Lowland creatures, who had sought refuge on higher ground, were waiting patiently for the water to recede. Deer were wading through the flooded fields. Beavers were busily collecting a trove of fallen branches. Geese honked in the sky before splashing down into a watery section of the forest.

Clearly, the animals were experts at survival.

Clearly, the robot was not.

Roz was crusted with mud and grit, so she gave herself another good cleaning, but that only revealed her dents and scratches. They were really starting to add up. She hardly resembled the perfect robot who had appeared on the shore just a week earlier.

The wilderness was taking a toll on poor Roz. So she felt something like relief when she spotted the quiet hole in the side of the mountain. It looked like a safe place for a robot. She stomped across the hillside and up to the cave, but never stopped to wonder what might be lurking within.

CHAPTER 14

THE BEARS

Roz stomped into the cave. And then she stomped right back out.

"Please stay away!" said the robot to the two bears who were now nipping at her heels. You see, when Roz stomped into the cave, she accidentally woke a brother and sister bear from their morning nap, which is never a good idea. And to make matters worse, bears have an instinct that drives them to attack when a creature runs away, especially if the creature running away is a mysterious, sparkling monster. So as the startled bears watched Roz stomping out of their cave, they really had no choice

at all. They simply had to take up the chase.

Roz tried her best to outrun the bears. She leaped over rocks and wove through trees and stomped across the mountainside at full speed. But the bears were young and strong and fast, and the robot still had so much to learn about moving through the wilderness. She never even saw the tree root. One moment she was stomping along, and the next moment she was flying through the air and thumping down onto a rotten log. Clumps of soft wood stuck to her side as she stood and faced her attackers.

Wouldn't you be afraid if two bears were charging toward you? Of course you would! Everyone would! Even the robot felt something like fear. Roz was programmed to take care of herself. She was pro-grammed to stay alive. And as the robot watched those bears charging toward her, she knew her life was in serious danger.

The bears slammed into Roz, knocking her against the trunk of a towering tree. Then one bear dove at her legs, and the other clawed at her chest. If only the robot had swung her fists or kicked her feet, she could have scared them off. One good bop in the nose would have sent them running. But the robot's programming would not allow her to be violent. Clearly, Roz was not designed to fight bears.

Powerful jaws chomped her arms. Sharp claws slashed her face. A massive head rammed her chest.

"Please stay away!" said the robot.

"*Roarrrr!*" said the sister bear.

"*Grrrrrr!*" said the brother bear.

And then the bears went in for the kill.

But the robot had vanished.

CHAPTER 15
THE ESCAPE

Using all the strength in her legs, Roz jumped straight up, high into the air, and landed on a tree branch overhead. The tree shook with the sudden weight of the robot, and then—*thunk thunk!*—two pinecones bounced off Roz, and a moment later—*thunk thunk!*—the same pinecones bounced off the bears below. The bears grunted with annoyance. This gave Roz an idea.

The robot's programming stopped her from being violent, but nothing stopped her from being annoying. So Roz plucked pinecones from the nearby branches and lobbed them down at the bears.

Thunk! Thunk! Thunk! Thunk!

Each pinecone bounced off its target with annoying accuracy and whipped the young bears into a frenzy.

"*Roarrrr!*" said the sister bear.

"*Grrrrrr!*" said the brother bear.

"I do not understand you, bears," said the robot.

Roz was about to unload a whole armful of annoying pinecones when a distant roar echoed through the forest. Back at the cave, the mother bear was calling for these two, and she did not sound happy. The young bears looked at each other. They knew they were in trouble. But before lumbering home, they glared up at Roz and snorted one last time. More than anything, they wanted to kill the robot.

CHAPTER 16

THE PINE TREE

Roz was in no hurry to leave the tree. She stayed on her branch long after the bears had gone, enjoying some peace and looking herself over.

In addition to bite marks and claw marks, the robot was also covered in dirt, which, of course, meant it was time for another cleaning. She was making good progress when she felt something sticky on her arm. The problem with sitting in a pine tree is that, eventually, the tree's sticky resin will find you. It always does. And it found Roz. The robot scrubbed and scraped at the resin, and soon her fingers were completely coated in the sticky stuff. Then it was all over her arms and her legs and her torso. And things were about to get even messier.

A robin swooped into the tree and began screeching and fluttering around Roz. The bird had recently finished

building herself a new nest. It was a little work of art, a delicate basket woven from grass and twigs and feathers, and it was right above the robot's head.

"*Screech! Screech!*" said the robin.

"I do not understand you, robin," said the robot.

The robin continued screeching and fluttering, and then—*splat*—she splattered her droppings across the robot's face. This bird was serious. So Roz scooted away, farther out on the branch, until she heard a quick, sharp *crack*. Before Roz knew what was happening, the tree branch snapped under her weight and she went crashing to the forest floor. She hit the ground hard and lay there as broken branches and pinecones and needles showered down on top of her. There was another *splat*. And then quiet returned to the forest.

CHAPTER 17

THE CAMOUFLAGED INSECT

Roz was a mess. She lay under the tree, covered in a heap of broken branches and pinecones and needles. She still hadn't removed the sticky resin from her body. And then there were the bird droppings. She was about to get up and give herself a rigorous cleaning when she noticed a peculiar twig. The twig was moving. It was crawling

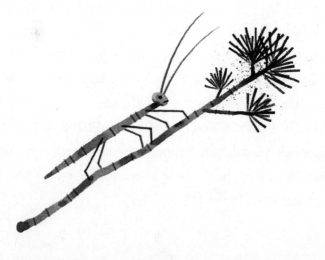

along one of the broken branches on the ground. With a gentle touch, the robot picked up the twig.

"Hello, stick insect, my name is Roz. You are very well camouflaged."

The stick insect's body was long and thin. He had the same shape and colors and markings as a real twig. But if you looked closely, you just might see two tiny eyes and two spindly antennae. The insect didn't make a sound, and he sat perfectly still. As still as the robot. The two of them sat still and silently stared at each other for a while.

"Thank you, stick insect," said Roz as she placed him back where she found him. "You have taught me an important lesson. I can see how camouflage helps you survive; perhaps it could help me survive also."

CHAPTER 18

THE CAMOUFLAGED ROBOT

As you know, reader, Roz had always liked to keep herself as clean as possible. But her desire to stay alive was stronger than her desire to stay clean, and our robot decided it was time she got dirty. Roz was going to camouflage herself.

She'd gotten the idea from the stick insect, but Roz quickly realized that camouflaging herself as a twig was out of the question. No, the robot would have to blend into the landscape itself. She began by smearing handfuls of thick mud over her entire body. Then she plucked ferns and grasses from the ground and sank their roots into her new muddy coating. She placed colorful flowers around her face to disguise her glowing eyes, and any bare patches were covered with tree leaves and strips of moss. Our robot now looked like a great tuft of plants

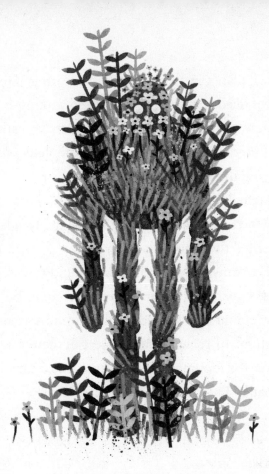

walking through the forest. She waited for darkness, and then she padded to the center of a clearing, nestled herself between some rocks, and became part of the landscape.

A few hours later, the sky was brightening, the fog was lifting, the nighttime animals were slinking home, and the daytime animals were beginning to stir. It was just an ordinary morning on the island. However, there was that new tuft of plants in that one forest clearing. Only the bees had noticed the tuft. They buzzed around it, completely unaware that the robot was hidden beneath. And so Roz sat there, right in the open yet completely unseen, and observed the wilderness around her.

She watched flowers slowly turn toward the sun.

She listened to rodents crawl through the weeds.

She smelled the moist, piney air.

She felt worms wiggle against her muddy sides.

A week later, the tuft of plants was gone, but there was a new clump of seaweed on the shore. A week after that, the clump of seaweed was gone, but there was a new bramble on the mountain. Then there was a new log on the riverbank. Then a new rock in the forest.

CHAPTER 19

THE OBSERVATIONS

Clouds scudded through the sky.

Spiders spun intricate webs.

Berries beckoned to hungry mouths.

Foxes stalked hares.

Mushrooms rose up from leaf litter.

Turtles plopped into ponds.

Moss spread across tree roots.

Vultures hunched over carcasses.

Ocean waves beat against the coastline.

Tadpoles became frogs, caterpillars became butterflies.

A camouflaged robot observed it all.

CHAPTER 20

THE LANGUAGE OF THE ANIMALS

It started with the birds. They had always been skittish when the robot was near. They would stare and screech and then scatter. But now that Roz was camouflaged, she could secretly observe their normal behavior, right up close.

Roz noticed chickadees fluttering through the same flowers and singing the same song every morning. She noticed a lark who swooped down to the same rock and sang the same song every afternoon. She noticed the same two magpies singing to each other from across the same meadow every evening. After weeks of robotically studying the birds, Roz knew what each bird would sing, and when they would sing, and eventually, why they would sing. The robot was beginning to understand the birds.

But she was also beginning to understand the porcupines and the salamanders and the beetles. She discovered that all the different animals shared one common language; they just spoke the language in different ways. You might say each species spoke with its own unique accent.

When Roz first listened to the chickadees, their songs had sounded like "TWEEE-tweedle! TWEEE-tweedle!" But now when the chickadees sang, Roz heard "Oh, what a lovely day it is! Oh, what a lovely day it is!"

Deer spoke mostly with their bodies. By simply turning her head, a doe could say to her family, "Let's look for clovers by the stream."

Snakes often hissed to themselves, things like "I know there's a tasty mouse around here sssssomewhere."

Bees said very little. They used their wings to buzz a few simple words, like *nectar* and *sun* and *hive*.

Frogs spent much of their time searching for each other. One would croak, "Where are you? I can't see you!" And then another would reply, "I'm over here! Follow my voice!"

When Roz first stomped across the island, the animal squawks and growls and chirps had sounded like nothing more than meaningless noises. But she no longer heard animal noises. Now she heard animal words.

CHAPTER 21

THE INTRODUCTION

There was an hour each morning, in the dim light of dawn, when all the island animals were safe. You see, long ago they had agreed not to hunt or harm one another during that hour. They called it the Dawn Truce. Most mornings, the island residents would gather in the Great Meadow and spend the hour chatting with friends. Of course, not everyone attended these gatherings. The bears had never made an appearance. And the vultures just circled high above. But on this particular morning, an unusually large group of animals had come out to discuss some important news.

"Settle down, everyone—I have something to say!" Swooper the owl hooted to the crowd from the lowest branch of a dead tree. "Last night I saw a mysterious creature right here in the Great Meadow. It seemed to be covered in grass, so I couldn't get a good look at it, but I think it may have been the monster."

Looks of concern swept over the crowd.

"What was the creature doing?" said Dart the weasel.

"It was speaking," said Swooper. "It kept repeating the same words over and over again. But each time it sounded a little different. At first it sounded like a cricket, and then it sounded like a raccoon, and then it sounded like an owl!"

"What was it saying?" said Digdown the groundhog.

"I could be mistaken," said Swooper, "but I think it was saying, 'Hello, my name is Roz.'"

The crowd began to chatter.

"Just where was this creature?" said Fink the fox.

Everyone turned as the owl slowly pointed his wing to a grassy lump in the meadow. It was a rather ordinary-looking grassy lump. Until it began to move.

As you probably guessed, that grassy lump was Roz. She had been there the whole time, camouflaged, watching, listening, and with all the animals looking at her she decided to introduce herself. The crowd stared in disbelief as the grassy lump started shaking and bulging upward and crumbling apart, and there was the robot! Then, using her body and voice, the robot spoke to the animals in their own language.

"Hello, my name is Roz."

The crowd gasped.

Swooper fluttered up from his branch and screeched, "It's the monster!"

"I am not a monster," said Roz. "I am a robot."

A flock of sparrows suddenly took off.

"Leave us alone!" squeaked Dart as he crouched low in the grass. "Return to whatever horrible place you've come from!"

"I come from here," said Roz. "I have spent my whole life on this island."

"Why haven't you spoken to us sooner?" screeched the owl, from higher up in the tree.

"I did not know the animal language until now," said the robot.

Crownpoint the buck had heard enough, and he slipped into the forest with his family.

"So what do you want from us?" growled Fink.

"I have observed that different animals have different ways of surviving," said the robot. "I would like each of you to teach me your survival techniques."

"I'm not going to help you!" screeched the owl, from the very top of the tree. "You seem so...unnatural!"

"The monster is just waiting to gobble us up!" shrieked Digdown. And the groundhog disappeared into a hole.

"I will not gobble anyone up," said Roz. "I have no need for food."

"You don't need food?" Fink relaxed a bit. "Well, I need food. And lots of it. Why don't you make yourself useful and find me some food?"

"What would you like me to do?" said Roz.

"Can you hunt?" The fox smiled at a hare on the far side of the gathering. "It's almost time for breakfast."

"I cannot hunt. But I could gather berries."

The fox's smile disappeared. "Berries? I'm hungry for meat, not berries! Good luck to you, Roz. You're gonna need it!" And the fox trotted away.

Roz looked up at the tree, but the owl had gone. And when the robot looked down again, she realized that everyone else had gone too.

CHAPTER 22
THE NEW WORD

A new word was spreading across the island. The word was *Roz*. Everyone was talking about the robot. And they wanted nothing to do with her.

"I don't think I'll ever feel comfortable knowing that Roz is on the prowl."

"I hope Roz camouflages herself as a rock. Forever."

"Shhh! There's Roz now! Let's get out of here!"

Roz wandered the island, covered in dirt and green growing things, and everywhere she went, she heard unfriendly words. The words would have made most creatures quite sad, but as you know, robots don't feel emotions, and in these moments that was probably for the best.

CHAPTER 23

THE WOUNDED FOX

"My face! My beautiful face! Somebody help!" Fink the fox was lying on a log, howling in pain, with a face full of long, sharp quills, when Roz appeared. "Isn't there anybody else who can help?"

"Would you like me to leave?" said the robot.

"No! Please don't go! I'll take what I can get."

"What happened?"

"I didn't think that porcupine could see me in the bushes, but when I went for his throat, suddenly there were quills in my face!"

"Why did you go for his throat?"

"Why do you think? Because I was hungry!"

"If you had not attacked the porcupine, you would not have quills in your face."

"Yes, Roz, I know that. But a fox has gotta eat! I just

didn't expect him to put up such a fight. Look! There are even quills in my paws! I can't walk! My face is numb! I could die if you don't help me!"

"What would you like me to do?" said the robot.

"I'd like you to pull out the quills!"

Roz calmly knelt beside Fink and said, "I will pull out the quills."

The robot started to tug on a quill, but it snapped off in her fingers. Fink yelped and said, "Pinch it closer to the skin!" So Roz pinched the broken quill closer to the skin, and then, very slowly, she pulled it out. The fox winced in pain and said through his teeth, "Please, Roz, pull them out faster. This is agony!"

Roz quickly tugged out another quill. Then another, and another. The fox lay perfectly still, eyes closed tightly, wind whistling through his nose, until every single quill had been removed and placed in a neat pile beside him.

Fink struggled to his feet. "Thanks, Roz. I...I owe you one." The fox smiled, briefly, and then he limped away.

CHAPTER 24

THE ACCIDENT

As Roz wandered through springtime, she saw all the different ways that animals entered the world. She saw birds guarding their eggs like treasures until the chicks finally hatched. She saw deer give birth to fawns who were up and running in a matter of minutes. Many newborns were greeted by loving families. Some were on their own from their very first breath. And, as you're about to find out, a few poor goslings would never even get a chance to hatch.

Roz was climbing down one of the forest cliffs when the accident happened. The wind started blowing out of the north, and suddenly clouds were rushing over the island. With the clouds came a spring shower. A downpour, actually. And there was our robot, clamping her hands onto a wet block of stone on the side of the cliff. But the block couldn't handle the extra weight. And as the heavy robot hung there, cracks suddenly shot through the stone and it started breaking apart. Down went the robot, plummeting into the treetops below. She crashed through branch after branch before finally hooking an arm around one. Then she dangled there, gently swinging as rocks roared past her on their way to the forest floor.

When the dust settled, Roz shimmied down the tree trunk. The ground was littered with broken rocks and splintered wood and pulverized shrubs. And within all that rubble was a goose nest that had been torn to shreds. Two dead geese and four smashed eggs lay among the carnage. The robot stared at them with her softly glowing eyes, and something clicked deep inside her computer brain. Roz realized she had caused the deaths of an entire family of geese.

CHAPTER 25
THE EGG

As Roz stood in the rain, staring down at those poor, lifeless geese, her sensitive ears detected a faint peeping sound coming from somewhere nearby. She followed the peeps over to a clump of wet leaves on the ground. And when she peeled back the leaves, she discovered a single perfect goose egg sunk in the mud.

"Mama! Mama!" peeped a tiny, muffled voice from within the egg.

The robot gently cradled the fragile thing in her hand. Without a family, the unhatched gosling inside would surely die. Roz knew that some animals had to die for others to live. That was how the wilderness worked. But would she allow her accident to cause the death of yet another gosling?

After a moment, the robot started to walk. Carefully

holding the egg, she moved through the forest and away from that sad scene. But she didn't get far before Fink burst out from the bushes.

"What happened?" The fox panted. "The whole forest was shaking!"

"There was an accident," said the robot. "I was climbing those cliffs when the rocks started to fall."

"You should be more careful," said Fink as he checked out the robot's new scrapes and dents. "I'll need your help if I ever have more porcupine trouble!"

"I will be more careful."

"What do you have there?" said Fink, looking up at Roz's hands.

"A goose egg."

"Oh! I love eggs! Can I eat it?"

"No."

"Please?"

"No."

"Why do you want it?" The fox scowled. "I thought you didn't eat food."

"You may not have this egg, Fink."

The fox sighed. He scratched his chin. And then he started sniffing the breeze. His nose had found the scent of the dead geese. "You can keep your egg!" he said as he trotted toward the cliffs. "I smell something better!"

The robot walked on through the misty forest for a long time, until she was standing beneath a sprawling oak tree. Roz placed the egg on a pad of moss. Then she snatched grass and twigs from the ground and delicately wove them together to make a little nest. She placed the egg inside the nest, placed the nest on her flat shoulder, and climbed up into the branches.

CHAPTER 26
THE PERFORMER

Up in the sprawling oak, the goose egg was peeping and wobbling around its nest.

"*Mama! Mama!*" said the egg.

"I am not your mother," said the robot.

The egg continued peeping and wobbling until nightfall, when the gosling inside settled down to sleep and the egg became quiet and still.

The robot was about to settle into her own kind of sleep when she heard something in the underbrush below. Roz peered down from the branches and saw weeds rustling in the moonlight. A creature was crawling past. But the creature stayed low, hiding in the darkest shadows, so that Roz couldn't see who it was. Roz wasn't the only one watching. A pair of furry ears rose up behind a log. The ears belonged to a very hungry badger. He lay in wait as the shadowy creature came closer and closer, and when the time was right, the badger pounced.

You might expect a creature under attack to run for her life, or to defend herself, or at the very least to scream. But when the badger pounced, this creature just rolled onto her back, stuck out her tongue, and died. Not only was she dead, she was rotten, and the badger's face twisted with disgust. "Blecch! What a stench!" He pawed at the stinky corpse a few times and then gave up. "No, thanks," he grumbled to himself. "I'd rather eat beetles." And the badger hurried off to find a less disgusting meal.

Had that mysterious creature been frightened to death? And how could her body possibly rot so quickly? Roz was confused. And the robot became considerably more confused an hour later, when the dead creature's ears began to flicker, her nose began to twitch, and she rolled onto her feet and went on her way as if nothing had happened.

The robot's voice called down from the tree. "Are you alive or are you dead?"

The creature's voice hissed up from the shadows. "Who's there? Why have you been watching me?"

"What you just did was unbelievable," said Roz. "I could not look away."

"Unbelievable? Really?" The creature's voice seemed to be softening. "I thought perhaps I overdid it when I stuck out my tongue."

"I was certain you were dead."

"Oh, what a lovely thing to say!"

"Were you dead?"

"Well, of course not! Nobody can actually come back from the dead. It was just an act!"

"I do not understand."

"It's simple. I knew that if I played dead and really laid it on thick, that old badger would be so disgusted that he'd run off. And that is exactly what happened. We opossums are natural performers, you know."

"So, you are an opossum." Roz's computer brain quickly retrieved any information it had on opossums. "You are a marsupial, and are nocturnal, and are known for mimicking the appearance and smell of dead animals when threatened."

"It's true, death scenes are my specialty," said the opossum. "But I have a wide dramatic range, believe me."

"I believe you."

"Have you done any acting?" said the opossum.

"I have not," said the robot.

"Well, you should! You might enjoy it. You can start by imagining the character you'd like to be. How do they move and speak? What are their hopes and fears? How do others react to them? Only when you truly understand a character can you become that character..."

The two odd creatures sat there, one in a tree, the other in the weeds, and talked about acting. The opossum went on and on about her various acting methods and her triumphant performances, and our robot absorbed every word.

"But why do you pretend to be something you are not?" said the robot.

"Because it's fun!" said the opossum. "And because

it helps me survive, as you just saw. You never know, it might help you survive too."

Soon, the robot's computer brain was humming with activity. Performing could be a survival strategy! If the opossum could pretend to be dead, the robot could pretend to be alive. She could act less robotic and more natural. And if she could pretend to be friendly, she might make some friends. And they might help her live longer, and better. Yes, this was an excellent plan.

Roz wasted no time and spoke her next words in the friendliest voice she could muster. "Madam marsupial, it would be a great honor and absolute privilege if you would kindly inform me of your name." Roz's friendly demeanor needed some work, but it was a start.

"Yes, of course!" said the opossum. "My name is Pinktail. And you are?"

Leaves gently shook as Roz climbed down from the tree. "It is a very lovely pleasure to make your acquaintance, my dear Pinktail." A moment later, the robot stepped into the moonlight. "My name is Roz."

"Oh my!" the opossum gasped. "You're the m-m-monster!"

"I am not a monster. I am a robot. And I am harmless."

"Harmless? Really? Well, you do seem rather gentle. And I heard someone say that you don't eat any food at all, which makes no sense, but hopefully it means you won't eat me?"

"I will not eat you," said the robot.

"I'm so glad to hear that," said the opossum. And a moment later, she too stepped into the moonlight. "It's nice to meet you, Roz." A weak smile appeared on Pinktail's pointy face.

Roz thought things were going really well. But she didn't know what to say next. Neither did Pinktail. So the two friendly creatures just stood there together and listened to the crickets for a while.

"Well, I should be on my way," said Pinktail at last. "Have a nice evening, Roz."

"Have the nicest evening, Pinktail. I shall look forward to the pleasure of encountering you again in the future. Soon, I hope. Farewell."

With that awkward good-bye, Pinktail slipped back into the weeds and Roz climbed back into the tree.

CHAPTER 27

THE GOSLING

Something was happening inside the goose egg.

Tap, tap, tap.

Tap, tap, tap.

Tap, tap, CRUNCH!

A tiny bill poked through the eggshell, peeped once, and then continued crunching away. The hole grew bigger and bigger, and then, like a robot breaking from a crate, the hatchling pulled himself out into the world.

He lay quietly in his nest with his eyes closed, surrounded by chips of broken shell. And when his eyes slowly winked open, the very first thing he saw was the robot looking back.

"Mama! Mama!" peeped the gosling.

"I am not your mother," said the robot.

"Mama! Mama!"

"I am not your mother."

"Food! Food!"

The gosling was hungry. Of course he was. So, using her friendliest voice, Roz said, "What would you like to eat, little darling?"

"Food!" was the only response. The hatchling was far too young to be helpful. Roz needed to find a grown goose. So she scooped up the nest with the gosling inside, placed it on her flat shoulder, and marched through the forest, searching for geese.

CHAPTER 28

THE OLD GOOSE

Ordinarily, the forest animals would have run away from the monster. But they were awfully curious why she was carrying a hatchling on her shoulder. And once Roz explained the situation, the animals actually tried to help. A frog pointed Roz up to the squirrels. A squirrel recommended that she speak with the magpies. And then a magpie sent them over to the beaver pond.

The ground grew soggier, the grass grew taller, and soon the robot and the gosling were looking across a wide, murky pond. Dragonflies buzzed through the reeds. Turtles sunned themselves on a log. Schools of small fish gathered in the shadows. And there, floating in the center of the pond, was an old gray goose.

"A very good morning to you!" the robot's friendly

voice boomed over the water. "I have an adorable little gosling with me!"

The goose just stared.

"I am in great need of your assistance!" said Roz. "Actually, the gosling is in need of your assistance!"

The goose didn't move.

"Food!" peeped the gosling. "Food! Food!"

That tiny voice was more than the old goose could bear, and she began gliding across the pond and squawking to the robot, "What are you doing with that hungry hatchling? Where are his parents?"

"There was a terrible accident," said Roz. "It was my fault. This gosling is the only survivor."

"If there was a terrible accident, why does your voice sound so cheerful?" The goose flapped her wings. "Are you sure you didn't *eat* his parents?"

"I am sure I did not eat his parents," said Roz, returning to her normal voice. "I do not eat anything, including parents."

The goose squinted at the robot. Then she said, "Do you know who his parents were?"

"I do not know."

"Well, they must have belonged to one of the other flocks on the island, because nobody in my flock is missing."

"Will you take the gosling?"

"I most certainly will not!" squawked the goose. "I can't take in every orphan I see! You say this is your fault? It seems to me that it's up to you to make things right."

"Mama! Mama!" peeped the gosling.

"I have tried to tell him that I am not his mother," said the robot. "But he does not understand."

"Well, you'll have to act like his mother if you want him to survive."

There was that word again—*act*. Very slowly, the robot was learning to act friendly. Maybe she could learn to act motherly as well.

"You do want him to survive, don't you?" said the goose.

"Yes, I do want him to survive," said the robot. "But I do not know how to act like a mother."

"Oh, it's nothing, you just have to provide the gosling with food and water and shelter, make him feel loved but don't pamper him too much, keep him away from danger, and make sure he learns to walk and talk and swim and fly and get along with others and look after himself. And that's really all there is to motherhood!"

The robot just stared.

"Mama! Food!" said the gosling.

"Now would probably be a good time to feed your son," said the goose.

"Yes, of course!" said the robot. "What should I feed him?"

"Give him some mashed-up grass. And if a few insects get in there, all the better."

Roz tore several blades of grass from the ground. She mashed them into a ball and then dropped the ball into the nest. The gosling shook his tail feathers and chewed his very first bites of food.

"By the way, my name is Loudwing," said the goose.

"Everyone already knows your name, Roz. But what's the gosling's name?"

"I do not know." The robot looked at her adopted son. "What is your name, gosling?"

"He can't name himself!" squawked Loudwing.

And then, with a loud burst of wingbeats, the goose fluttered up from the pond and landed right on Roz's head. Water streamed down the robot's dusty body as Loudwing leaned over the nest.

"Oh dear, he certainly is a tiny thing," said Loudwing. "He must be a runt. I'll warn you, Roz—runts usually don't last very long. And with you for a mother, it'll take a miracle for him to survive. I'm sorry, but it's the truth. However, the gosling still deserves a name. Let's see here. His bill is an unusually bright color. It's actually quite lovely. If I were his mother, I'd call him Brightbill, but you're his mother, so it's up to you."

"His name will be Brightbill," said Roz as the goose fluttered back to the water. "And we will live by this pond, where he can be around other geese. I will find us a sturdy tree nearby."

"You will do no such thing!" The goose flapped her wings. "A tree is no place for a gosling! Brightbill needs to live on the ground, like a normal goose."

Loudwing sized up the robot. "I suppose you two will need a rather large home. You'd better speak with Mr. Beaver. He can build anything. He's a little gruff at times, but if you're extra friendly, I'm sure he'll help you out. And if he gives you trouble, remind him that he owes me a favor."

CHAPTER 29
THE BEAVERS

Every day, the beavers swam along their dam, inspecting and repairing it. The wall of wood and mud allowed only a trickle of water to pass through, and it had turned a narrow stream into the wide pond that many animals now called home.

As Roz and Brightbill walked around the pond, they passed hundreds of chewed-up tree stumps, proof that the beavers needed a constant supply of wood. And this gave Roz an idea.

The robot swung her flattened hand, and the sounds of chopping wood echoed across the water. They were soon replaced by the sounds of footsteps and shaking leaves as the robot carefully walked along the beaver dam with a gosling on her shoulder and a freshly cut tree in her hands. The beavers floated beside their lodge and stared at the bizarre sight with open mouths until Mr. Beaver slapped his broad tail on the water, which meant "Stop right there!"

The robot stopped. "Hello, beavers, my name is Roz, and this is Brightbill. Please do not be frightened. I am not dangerous." She held out the tree. "I have brought you a gift! I thought perhaps you could use this in your beautiful dam."

"No, thanks," said Mr. Beaver. "I have a strict policy never to accept gifts from monst—"

"Don't be ridiculous," interrupted Mrs. Beaver. "We can't let a perfectly good birch go to waste!"

"I'm afraid I must insist!" said Mr. Beaver.

Mrs. Beaver turned to her husband. "Remember how you asked me to point out when you're being stubborn and rude? Well, you're being stubborn and rude!" Then she turned back to Roz. "Thank you, monster. If you'd be so kind as to drop the tree in the water, we'll take it from there."

"I am not a monster." Roz tossed the tree like a twig. "I am a robot." The tree smacked against the water and sent the beavers bobbing up and down.

Just then, Brightbill started peeping. "Mama! Hungry!" So Roz dropped a ball of grass into the nest.

"The gosling thinks you're his mother?" came a quiet voice. It was Paddler, Mr. and Mrs. Beaver's son.

"His real mother is dead," said Roz. "So I have adopted him."

There was a brief silence. Then Paddler looked up at Roz and said, "You're a very good robot to take care of Brightbill."

Mr. Beaver sighed. "Yes, yes, that's very good of you, Roz. But I don't understand what any of this has to do with us."

"My son and I need a home, and Loudwing said you would help us build one."

"Of course she did," Mr. Beaver muttered to himself. "Loudwing gets me out of one lousy jam, and I spend the rest of my days doing her favors."

Mrs. Beaver glared at her husband.

"Sorry," he said, realizing he was being stubborn and rude again. "Stay right there, Roz. We need to have a family meeting."

The three beavers slipped under the water, and a moment later their muffled voices could be heard inside the lodge. The robot stood on the dam and patiently waited with her son.

"Mama! Mama!"

"Yes, Brightbill, I am trying to act like a good mother."

A ripple, and Mr. Beaver's head appeared above the water. "If you bring us four more trees—good, healthy ones—maybe I'll have time to help you and the gosling."

"That is wonderful!" said the robot. "We will be right back!"

CHAPTER 30
THE NEST

"*I've built my fair share* of lodges over the years." Mr. Beaver stood at the water's edge. "But I can't say I've ever built one for a robot and a gosling. So, just what exactly do you need?"

"We need a lodge big enough for us both," said Roz. "It should be comfortable and safe. And it should be near the pond."

"How long do you plan on living in this lodge?"

"I do not know."

"Then we'd better make sure it's strong and sturdy." Mr. Beaver stroked his whiskers as he thought. "Do you plan on having friends over? The missus loves to entertain guests."

"I do not have any friends."

"No friends? Well, you seem pretty likable for a

monster. I mean, a robot. But if you want my advice, you should grow yourself a garden. Your neighbors won't be able to resist fresh herbs and berries and flowers. Just you wait and see! So we'll make sure there's a place for a garden, and we'll give your lodge some extra space for all the friends you'll be hosting." The beaver winked. "We also need to find a way to keep your lodge comfortable when it's cold outside. Our lodge is heated by our own bodies. But I think we'll have to find another way to heat yours."

The beaver and the robot thought about heat for a while. The first thing that came to Roz's mind was the sun. But then she remembered the hot sparks she had felt while sliding down the mountain peak.

"I could heat our lodge with fire," she said.

Mr. Beaver blinked his little eyes.

"I will need to experiment," Roz continued. "But I think there is a way."

"You go right ahead, Roz," said the beaver. "But would you try not to burn down the entire forest?"

"Do not worry. I will be careful."

"Let's move on." Mr. Beaver sighed. "The next order of business is to find a site for your lodge. That meadow across the water would be perfect, but the hares will have a fit if we try to build there. I think we should clear out some trees and build right in the forest. And I know just the place!"

The beaver took them along the water and up to a dense section of forest that jutted into the pond.

"It needs some work," said Mr. Beaver, trudging through the thick weeds, "but this ought to do the job."

"Yes, this ought to do the job," said Roz, in her friendliest voice.

"Job!" said Brightbill.

Mr. Beaver was incredibly skilled at taking down trees, but even he couldn't keep up with Roz's powerful chopping hands. So he let the robot do the hard work. He pointed out the trees and shrubs that needed to go, and Roz started hacking away. By sunset, they were standing in a newly cleared site, and they had more than enough wood to build the lodge.

"You did some fine work today, Roz." Mr. Beaver yawned. "I'll return in the morning, and we'll pick up right where we left off."

"What would you like me to do?" said the robot.

"Tonight? So you still feel like working, do you? Very good! Well, you can start by digging out these tree stumps. And you can collect all those large, flat stones over there.

And you can smooth down this patch of dirt so we have a level place to build. That should keep you busy!"

The next morning, Mr. Beaver returned to find that Roz had been very busy indeed. All the tree stumps had been dug up, and their holes filled in with dirt. Twenty large stones had been stacked. And the ground was now perfectly level. But what most astonished Mr. Beaver was that Roz and Brightbill were huddled around a small crackling campfire.

Mr. Beaver moved his lips, but no words came out.

"Brightbill was cold last night," said Roz. "So I taught myself how to make a fire."

"But—but—but *how*?"

"I discovered that when I strike these two stones together, they create sparks, like this. I directed sparks onto dry leaves and wood until they ignited. Once I had a fire, it was easy to keep it going. And if I need to put it out, I can just add water!"

Mr. Beaver sat and warmed his paws. "I've never seen fire in such a neat little bundle." He stared into the flames. "I've only seen it blazing through the forest, burning everything in its path. But this is marvelous!" He took another minute to enjoy the warmth. Then he and the robot got back to work.

Mr. Beaver asked Roz to dig a trench here, to place large stones there, to arrange logs this way, to smear mud that way. Birds and squirrels perched in the trees and watched the new lodge take shape. It resembled the beaver lodge, but it was larger, a great dome of wood and mud and leaves. A simple opening in the wall served as the entrance, and the door was nothing more than a heavy stone that the robot could slide out of the way.

Inside, the lodge was one big, round room. The arched ceiling was high enough that Roz could stand upright. A fire pit was set into the center of the floor, and a mesh of thin branches above acted as a vent. Long stones lined the interior walls, like benches, and were covered with thick cushions of moss. There was even a hole for storing food and water for Brightbill.

"You've got yourself a beautiful pond-view property!" said Mr. Beaver. "What are you going to name it?"

"I do not understand."

"Why, a beautiful lodge like this deserves a name! We call our lodge Streamcatcher."

The robot's computer brain didn't take long. "The lodge is for Brightbill. Brightbill is a bird. Birds live in nests. Could we call this lodge the Nest?"

"Huzzah!" squeaked the beaver. "The Nest is a fine name for your lodge!"

"Nest! Nest!" laughed Brightbill.

They stood outside the Nest and admired their handiwork until Mr. Beaver's belly began to grumble. "That sound means it's time for me to go get dinner."

"Thank you very much for your help," said Roz. "We could not have done this without you."

"You're quite welcome!" said Mr. Beaver, smiling. "For your garden you'll want to speak with Tawny, the doe who lives over the hill. She'll know just what to do. And now if you'll excuse me, I have to hurry home before Paddler eats all the best leaves. Enjoy your first night in the Nest!"

CHAPTER 31
THE FIRST NIGHT

The stars were out. A fire was crackling in the fire pit. Roz and Brightbill were settling into their first night in their new home.

"This lodge is where we will live from now on." The robot plucked her son from his little woven nest and placed him on the floor. "I hope you like it."

The gosling did like it. He liked that it was big and warm and peaceful. And he liked knowing that the forest and the pond were just outside. He waddled around, peeping to himself and exploring every little corner of the lodge until it was time for bed. His mother carefully laid him on a soft cushion of moss. But he didn't want to sleep there. So she put him back in his little nest, but he didn't want to sleep there either.

Brightbill looked up and said, "Mama, sit!"

Roz sat down.

Then he said, "Mama, hold!"

Roz held him. The robot's body may have been hard and mechanical, but it was also strong and safe. The gosling felt loved. His eyes slowly winked closed. And he spent the whole night quietly sleeping in his mother's arms.

CHAPTER 32

THE DEER

The deer family did not run from the sound of snapping twigs and crunching leaves. They had heard all about Roz and Brightbill, and they knew there was nothing to fear. Crownpoint stood before his doe and his three spotted fawns, and the family watched as the robot approached with the gosling on her shoulder.

"Hello, deer, my name is Roz, and this is Brightbill. We are looking for a doe named Tawny."

Crownpoint moved aside, and the doe silently stepped forward.

"Mr. Beaver helped us build a lodge," said Roz, "and he thought you might help us grow a garden."

"Mr. Beaver helped you?" came Tawny's gentle voice. "You must have done something for the beavers."

"I brought them freshly cut trees," said Roz.

Tawny looked at Crownpoint, and the buck slowly nodded.

"I will help you grow a garden," said the doe to the robot, "if you will let my family eat from it."

The robot nodded in agreement. And then she quietly led Tawny back to the Nest.

CHAPTER 33
THE GARDEN

After inspecting the grounds, Tawny asked Roz to remove all the dried brambles and weeds and leaves from the garden area. She asked her burrowing friends, the moles and the groundhogs, to dig through the dirt and loosen the soil. And then she asked all the neighbors to do something rather peculiar.

"Please leave your droppings around the Nest! The more droppings, the richer the soil, the healthier the garden."

As you can imagine, Tawny's request got everyone's attention. The place was soon crawling with woodland creatures curious to hear more about the garden project. And just like that, the robot was meeting her neighbors. The plan to help her make friends was already starting to work.

There was a festive feeling around the Nest that day. Animals were coming and going and chatting and laughing. After some pleasant conversation, each neighbor would choose their spot, leave their droppings, and be on their way. And always with a smile.

"We're happy to help!" said two smiling weasels after finishing up their business.

"It was our pleasure!" said a flock of smiling sparrows before they flew away.

"I shouldn't be much longer, now," said a smiling turtle as he slowly made his contribution.

As all this was going on, Roz walked around and thanked everyone. "I am not capable of defecating," she explained, "so your droppings are most appreciated!"

Once the grounds were fertilized, it was time for the plants. Tawny brought Roz and Brightbill out to a lush meadow. The robot sank her fingers into the ground and felt the spongy layer of roots below the grass. Slowly, carefully, she rolled up wide strips of sod, exposing the dark, wormy soil. She carried the rolls back to the Nest and spread them out to make a patchy lawn. Then she transplanted clumps of wildflowers and clovers and berries and shrubs and herbs until the Nest was surrounded by a scraggly collection of plants.

"It's not much to look at now," said Tawny, "but the grass will grow into these gaps, and the flowers and bushes should perk up in a few days. I'll return soon to make sure it's all taking root. Before long this will be a lovely, wild garden."

CHAPTER 34
THE MOTHER

Like most goslings, Brightbill followed his mother everywhere. He was a slow, tottering little thing, but Roz was rarely in a hurry, and together they loved meandering along the forest paths and around the banks of the pond. However, they spent most of their time right in their own garden. You see, the garden was no longer scraggly. Thanks to the robot's careful attention, it was now bursting with colors and scents and flavors. Clearly, Roz was designed to work with plants.

"Oh, Roz, you've been busy!" said Tawny as her family grazed on the wonderland of growing things. "This garden is glorious! You'll be seeing quite a lot of us around here."

Tawny meant what she said. Each morning, around daybreak, Roz and Brightbill would hear quiet footsteps outside the Nest. And there would be Tawny and Crownpoint and their fawns, Willow, Thistle, and Brook, happily nibbling on the garden.

The deer weren't the only regular visitors. The beavers became quite fond of gnawing on a certain hardy shrub at the edge of the garden. Digdown, the old groundhog, popped up to munch on berries. Broadfoot, the giant bull moose, came by to chew on tree shoots. And of course bees and butterflies were there every day, happily floating through the flowers. There always seemed to be friendly animals hanging around the garden.

It was amazing how differently everyone treated Roz these days. Animals who once ran from the robot in fear now stopped by the Nest just to spend time with her. The neighbors smiled and waved whenever Roz and Brightbill wandered past. And at the Dawn Truce, the other mothers were eager to share their parenting advice.

"Make sure Brightbill gets plenty of rest. A tired gosling is a cranky gosling!"

"When the wind starts blowing from the north, you must immediately get Brightbill to safety. North winds always bring bad weather."

"You'll never be the perfect mother, so just do the best you can. All Brightbill really needs is to know you're doing your best."

No gosling ever had a more attentive mother. Roz was always there, ready to answer her son's questions, or to play with him, or to rock him to sleep, or to whisk him away from danger. With a computer brain packed full of parenting advice, and the lessons she was learning on her own, the robot was actually becoming an excellent mother.

CHAPTER 35

THE FIRST SWIM

"Good afternoon, you two!" said Loudwing as she waddled into the garden. "Remember me, Brightbill?"

"Loudwing! Loudwing!"

"Very good!" The old goose giggled. "Now, Roz, do you know what tomorrow is? Tomorrow is Swimming Day! The day when all the parents take their goslings out on the pond for the first time. And you simply must bring Brightbill."

"Swim! Swim!" said the gosling, shaking his tail feathers.

"Brightbill can go," said Roz, "but I cannot swim. I cannot go on the pond with him. I will not be able to protect him."

"Who'd have thought a big thing like you would be afraid of a little water?" Loudwing laughed. "Well, don't you worry about Brightbill; he'll be safe in the flock. And he's going to have so much fun swimming with the other goslings! We begin at sunrise, so don't be late! See you in the morning!" And with that, the goose plopped into the water and glided away.

"Swim! Swim!" said the gosling.

"Yes, Brightbill," said the robot, staring at the pond. "Swim, swim."

Early the next morning, peeps and honks and splashes began echoing across the calm water. Roz and Brightbill followed a trail through the fog and over to a beach that was crawling with fluffy goslings and proud parents.

Roz took a few steps into the water, and her Survival Instincts immediately flared up. The robot's computer brain knew that if water got inside her body, it could do serious damage. And so as the other parents began swimming across the pond, Roz stood safely in the shallows and watched.

Brightbill ran up and down the beach with the other goslings, peeping and laughing and pretending to be afraid of the tiny waves. When one wave finally pulled him in, he felt his body floating on top of the water. A big smile appeared on the gosling's face. Clearly, Brightbill was designed to swim.

"Very good, Brightbill!" said Loudwing as she floated past. "You're a natural!"

"Yes, Brightbill, you are a natural!" said Roz, trying to sound like a good mother.

Loudwing rounded up all the goslings and gave them a quick swimming lesson. "Remember, everyone, paddle your feet evenly to swim in a straight line. Paddle with your right foot to go left, and paddle with your left foot to go right. Try it out and join the rest of us when you're ready. Happy Swimming Day!"

Loudwing and the other adult geese calmly glided toward the center of the pond. A jumble of goslings tried to keep up with them. The youngsters jostled and splashed and peeped with excitement, and gradually they paddled in the direction of their parents.

Only Brightbill lagged behind. "Mama swim?"

Roz pointed to the flock. "I cannot swim. Go have fun with the other geese. You will be safe with them."

The gosling took a deep breath. Then he shook his tail feathers and paddled his feet and set out on his very first swim. He drifted too far to the left. Then he drifted too far to the right. But his feet just kept paddling until he caught up to the other goslings.

Roz spent the morning watching her son swim around and around the pond. And as she watched him, she felt something like gratitude. Thanks to Brightbill, the robot now had friends and shelter and help. Thanks to Brightbill, the robot had become better at surviving. In a way, Roz needed Brightbill as much as Brightbill needed Roz. Which was precisely why she felt such concern when the mood on the pond suddenly changed.

One moment everything was tranquil, and the next moment the geese were in a panic. Something was violently sloshing through the group. It was Rockmouth, the giant, toothy pike. The fish had been a problem in the pond for as long as anyone could remember, but he'd never attacked goslings before. All the parents immediately went to protect their young—all the parents except Roz. The robot could only stand in the shallows and watch as her son left the other geese behind and desperately swam toward his mother.

"Swim to me, Brightbill! Quickly!"

The gosling kicked as fast as he could. But alone on the water, he made an easy target. The pond rippled as Rockmouth slashed below the surface.

"Mama! Help!" squeaked Brightbill.

The robot was terribly conflicted. Part of her knew she had to help her son, but another part knew she had to stay out of deep water. Her body lurched forward and then backward, again and again, as she struggled to make a decision.

And then Loudwing came to the rescue.

"Rockmouth, don't you dare harm that little darling!" The old goose fluttered over and splashed down right on top of the fish. "Leave…him…alone!" She pecked and kicked and beat her wings against the fish until he surrendered to the murky depths of the pond.

Loudwing escorted Brightbill back to the beach, and a minute later the gosling was in his mother's arms, safe and sound.

"Rockmouth isn't as dangerous as he seems," said the goose, out of breath. "But I think that's enough swimming for one day."

CHAPTER 36

THE GOSLING GROWS

Brightbill soon forgot about the incident with Rockmouth, and he spent his mornings cruising around the pond with the other goslings. He was becoming a great little swimmer. He was also becoming a great little speaker.

"Hello, my name is Brightbill!" he said to anyone who would listen.

The gosling was small for his age, and he always would be, but he was growing bigger and stronger by the day. His increasing size was matched by his increasing appetite. He gobbled down grass and berries and nuts and leaves. Sometimes he'd snack on little insects. If it was edible, Brightbill would eat it. And even if it wasn't edible, he might eat it anyway. Roz felt something like fright the time she saw Brightbill swallowing pebbles on the beach. She was holding him upside down, hoping the pebbles would fall out of his mouth, when Loudwing stepped in.

"Put the gosling down," said the goose with a laugh. "It's perfectly natural for Brightbill to eat a few pebbles. They'll help him digest his food. But not too many, okay, little one?"

Like most youngsters, Brightbill was incredibly curious. He explored the garden and the pond and the forest floor. And he would occasionally explore neighboring homes. He'd wander down some hole in the ground and say to whoever was there, "Hello, my name is Brightbill!" Then a long robot arm would reach in and pull the gosling back outside. "Sorry to bother you," Roz would say, in her friendliest voice.

The mother and son slipped into a good nighttime routine. While the gosling slept, the robot might tend the fire if it was cool out, or gently fan him if it was warm. If he woke up hungry or thirsty, Roz brought him food or water. And whenever he had nightmares, she was always there to rock him back to sleep.

CHAPTER 37

THE SQUIRREL

A small squirrel was scurrying through the garden. Brightbill had never seen her before. He peered out from the Nest and watched her bounce across the lawn. After a minute of spying, the gosling shook his tail feathers and waddled outside. "Hello, my name is Brightbill!"

The squirrel froze. Then she slowly turned around. And then she started to talk.

"Hi Brightbill my name is Chitchat and I'm a twelve-and-a-half-week-old squirrel and I'm new around here and your home is really big and round and I don't understand why smoke sometimes comes out of it..."

Reader, I'm not quite sure how Chitchat got enough air into her lungs to go on like that. And I'm not quite sure how Brightbill had the patience to listen. But he

stood there and politely nodded as Chitchat rambled on and on and on.

"...and sometimes I see you waddling behind your funny-looking mother and you seem so nice that I thought I'd come down and introduce myself but now I'm nervous and I'm talking too much and my name is Chitchat I think I said that already."

There was a pleasant silence.

Brightbill stood on one foot for a moment.

Then the gosling took a deep breath and said, "It's very nice to meet you Chitchat I don't think you talk too much I think you talk just enough and I like you so let's be friends."

A big smile appeared on the squirrel's tiny face. For once, Chitchat was speechless.

CHAPTER 38

THE NEW FRIENDSHIP

Chitchat wasn't speechless for long. She'd already been alive for a whole twelve and a half weeks, and she wanted to tell Brightbill about every exciting thing, and every boring thing, that had ever happened to her. And so, as the new friends played and explored and ate together, the squirrel shared her stories.

"I was born on the other side of the hill and then last week I decided I was ready to build my first drey which is what you call a squirrel nest and now I live in that tree with the weird bump in its trunk," she said while the two of them kicked pebbles into the pond.

"One time a weasel chased me through the treetops until he missed a branch and fell all the way down and crashed into a bush and walked away all wobbly and he never bothered me again," she said while the two of them crawled through a hollow log.

"Eww gross I saw you eat that ant one time I ate a gnat by accident and I didn't like it at all I mostly eat acorns and bark and tree buds and sometimes the yummy berries that grow in your garden," she said while the two of them took a snack break.

But Chitchat was as good a listener as she was a talker. And whenever it was Brightbill's turn to speak, she'd keep quiet and hang on his every word.

Do you know who enjoyed their conversations most of all? Our robot Roz. The protective mother was never far away, and she felt something like amusement at the silly conversations she overheard, and she felt something like happiness that her son had made such a good friend.

CHAPTER 39

THE FIRST FLIGHT

Brightbill had spent his entire life by the pond, and he was becoming very curious about what lay beyond his neighborhood. So one day his mother said to him, "Let us go for a walk, and I will show you more water than you can possibly imagine."

Roz placed the gosling on her flat shoulder, and the two of them set off across the island. They marched out of the forest, crossed the Great Meadow, and climbed uphill until they were at the top of the island's western ridge. Before them was a grassy slope that descended all the way to the dark, choppy waves that surrounded the island.

"That is a lot of water," said the wide-eyed gosling. "I'm a good swimmer, but I'm not good enough to swim across that pond."

"That is not a pond," said the robot. "That is an ocean.

I doubt any bird could swim across an ocean."

Waves rolled in from the horizon.

Seagulls circled above the shore.

A steady breeze blew up the slope.

Brightbill's yellow fluff had recently changed over to a coat of silky brown feathers, and he spread his feathery wings into the breeze. And then—

"Mama, look!" For the briefest of moments, the wind lifted Brightbill off the ground. But he quickly tipped backward and thumped into the soft grass. "I was flying!" he squeaked.

"That was not flying," said Roz, looking back at her upside-down son.

"Well, I was almost flying. I'm gonna try again!"

"I have observed many birds in flight," said Roz. "Sometimes they flap their wings quickly, and other times they fly without flapping at all. They spread their wings and soar on the wind."

"So I was soaring?" said Brightbill.

"Almost. There, look at that soaring seagull. It seems like she is not doing anything, but if you look closer, you will notice that she is making small adjustments with her wings and tail. I think you should try adjusting your wings in the wind, like her."

Brightbill hopped onto a rock and opened his wings wide. "The wind is pushing me backward!"

"Change the angle of your wings," said his mother. "Let us see what happens when they slice through the air."

Brightbill slowly angled his wings downward. The more he turned them, the less the wind pushed him backward. And just as his wings leveled off—

"Mama, look!" he squeaked as his feet left the ground. "I'm soaring! I'm soaring!" He hovered there for a second, rising a little higher than before, and then he sailed backward into the soft grass again.

The gosling kept hopping onto the rock and kept riding the wind and kept tumbling into the grass, until he started to find his wings. With each attempt he floated a little higher and a little longer, and finally Brightbill really *did* soar. He lifted high into the air and hung there, floating. He turned his wings down and felt himself drop. He wiggled his tail feathers and felt himself veering back and forth.

"I'm a natural!" he squeaked.

"You are doing very well," said Roz. "But you need to keep practicing."

And so they spent the afternoon practicing up on the ridge. Once Brightbill was comfortable soaring, he tried flapping his wings. He flapped high into the air. He flapped in straight lines. He flapped around and around in circles. A big smile appeared on the gosling's face. Clearly, Brightbill was designed to fly.

"I'm flying, Mama! I'm really flying!"

"You are flying!" said the robot. "Very good!"

Brightbill was now a real flier. But all that flying had worn him out. He lowered himself toward the ground and tumbled into the grass one last time. His landings still needed some work.

Roz placed Brightbill on her shoulder and headed back to the Nest.

"I can't believe I can fly now, Mama," said Brightbill in his sleepy voice. "I just wish...I just wish you could fly with me."

And then the gosling's words were replaced by his quiet, steady breathing.

CHAPTER 40
THE SHIP

Brightbill was a flying fanatic, and his favorite place to fly was up on the grassy ridge. The robot and the gosling liked to spend afternoons up there, working on the finer points of flying. And it was on one such afternoon that they noticed something mysterious far out at sea.

Brightbill spiraled down to his mother, flopped onto the grass, and pointed to the horizon. "Mama, what is that thing?"

Roz's computer brain found the right word. "That is a ship."

"What's a ship?"

"A ship is a large vessel used for ocean transport."

Brightbill's face scrunched up with confusion. "Used by who?"

"I do not know."

It was the first ship either of them had ever laid eyes on. From that distance, it looked as though it were moving slowly, but it was actually racing through the waves. From that distance, it looked as though it were small, but it was actually one of the largest ships ever built. The robot and the gosling watched it crawl across the ocean until it finally disappeared to the south.

Where had the ship come from? Where was it going? Who was on board? Roz and Brightbill had many questions but no answers.

CHAPTER 41
THE SUMMER

On clear summer days, Roz and Brightbill and Chitchat liked to go exploring. They investigated the island's sandy southern point. They marveled at the rainbows that curved up from the waterfall. They surveyed the forest from the branches of tall trees. They met new friendly creatures, and sometimes they met new unfriendly creatures. But the only creatures they had to worry about were the bears.

One time, they came upon a bear fishing in the river, and Roz whispered, "You know what to do." Brightbill flew up and away, Chitchat scurried home through the treetops, and Roz melted into the landscape as only she could. Later, they met back at the Nest and told the neighbors all about their brush with danger.

On dreary summer days, they would stay inside. Roz

asked Brightbill and Chitchat about dreaming and about flying and about eating and about all the things they could do that she could not. But the youngsters had too much energy to sit still for very long. They spent one drizzly afternoon kicking acorns around the Nest. Chitchat piled them up, and then Brightbill swung his big foot and the acorns went flying. The little friends chased the acorns as they bounced and rolled and spun across the floor. Then they made a new pile and kicked them again. Sometimes an acorn would bounce off Roz's body—*clang!*—and everyone would laugh and giggle together. Even Roz laughed. "Ha ha haaa!" said the robot, trying to act natural.

On clear summer evenings,

they would sit outside and watch fireflies twinkling around the pond. Then they'd lie back and gaze up at the darkening sky.

"That big circle is the moon," said Chitchat. "And those little lights are called stars and one time I tried to count them all but I can only count to ten so I just kept counting to ten over and over and I have no idea how many stars there are but I know it's more than ten."

"They are not all stars," said Roz. "Some of them are planets."

"What's a planet?" said Chitchat.

"A planet is a celestial body orbiting a star."

"What does 'celestial' mean?"

"Celestial means something that is in outer space."

"What's outer space?"

"Outer space is the universe outside the atmosphere of our planet."

"What's the universe?"

"The universe is everything and everywhere."

"Oh, so the universe is our island?"

None of them would ever really understand the universe, including Roz. Her computer brain knew only so much. She could talk about the earth and the sun and the moon and the planets, and a few stars, and not much else.

The night sky was full of streaking, shimmering, and blinking lights that she simply couldn't identify. Clearly, Roz was not designed to be an astronomer.

On dreary summer evenings, Roz and Brightbill would curl up together, just the two of them, and listen to the rain pattering on the roof of the Nest. The robot would tell stories of annoying pinecones and terrible storms and camouflaged insects. But the sound of rain always made Brightbill sleepy, and he'd be out before his mother could ever finish a story.

CHAPTER 42

THE STRANGE FAMILY

It was a sweltering afternoon, and the heat had put everyone in a bad mood. Roz was standing in the shade watching her son out on the water. The other goslings were teasing him about something when they suddenly burst into laughter, and Brightbill turned and hurried home with a stormy expression on his face. He stomped into the garden and right past his mother without saying a word.

"What is wrong, Brightbill?" said Roz as she followed her son into the Nest.

"Nothing!" he squawked. "Leave me alone!"

"Tell me what is wrong."

"I don't want to talk about it!"

"Maybe I can help."

"Mama, the other goslings were making fun of me."

"What did they say?"

"They called you a monster and then laughed at me for having a monster mother."

"They should know by now that I am not a monster. Would you like me to talk to them?"

"*No!* Don't do that! That'll just make things worse."

The robot sat next to her son.

"Mama, I know you're a robot. But I don't understand what a robot is."

"A robot is a machine. I was not born. I was built."

"Who built you?"

"I do not know. I do not remember being built. My very first memory is waking up on the northern shore of this island."

"Were you smaller back then?" said the gosling.

"No, I have always been this size." Roz looked down at her weathered body. "However, I used to be shiny, like the surface of the pond. I used to stand straighter than a tree trunk. I used to speak a different language. I have not grown bigger, but I have changed very much."

The robot wanted to explain things to her son, but the truth was that she understood very little about herself. It was a mystery how she had come to life on the rocky shore. It was a mystery why her computer brain knew certain things but not others. She tried to answer

Brightbill's questions, but her answers only left him more confused.

"What do you mean, you're not alive?" squawked Brightbill.

"It is true," said Roz. "I am not an animal. I do not eat or breathe. I am not alive."

"You move and talk and think, Mama. You're definitely alive."

It was impossible for such a young goose to understand technical things like computer brains and batteries and machines. The gosling was much better at understanding natural things like islands and forests and parents.

Parents. The word suddenly left Brightbill feeling uneasy. "You're not my real mother, are you?"

"There are many kinds of mothers," said the robot. "Some mothers spend their whole lives caring for their young. Some lay eggs and immediately abandon them. Some care for the offspring of other mothers. I have tried to act like your mother, but no, I am not your birth mother."

"Do you know what happened to my birth mother?"

Roz told Brightbill about that fateful day in spring. About how the rocks had fallen and only one egg had survived. About how she'd put the egg in a nest and carried it away. About how she'd watched over the egg until a tiny gosling hatched. Brightbill listened carefully until she finished.

"Should I stop calling you Mama?" said the gosling.

"I will still act like your mother, no matter what you call me," said the robot.

"I think I'll keep calling you Mama."

"I think I will keep calling you son."

"We're a strange family," said Brightbill, with a little smile. "But I kind of like it that way."

"Me too," said Roz.

CHAPTER 43
THE GOSLING
TAKES OFF

It must be hard to have a robot for a mother. I think the hardest part for Brightbill was all the mystery that surrounded Roz. Where had she come from? What was it like to be a robot? Would she always be there for him?

These questions filled the gosling's mind, and his feelings for his mother swung between love and confusion and anger. I'm sure many of you know what that's like. Roz could sense that Brightbill was struggling, and so she spent a lot of time talking with him about families and geese and robots.

"There are other robots on the island?" said the gosling during one of their talks. He'd been sitting beside his mother in the garden, but now stood and faced her.

"Yes, there are others on the island," said Roz, "but they are inoperative."

"Inoperative?"

"For a robot, being inoperative is like being dead."

"Where are the dead robots?"

"They are on the northern shore."

"I want to see them!"

"I do not think that is a good idea."

"Why not?"

"You are still a gosling. You are too young to see dead robots. I will take you to see them when you are older."

"Mama, I'm not a gosling anymore!" Brightbill puffed out his chest. "I'm already four months old!"

"I am sorry," said Roz. "But you cannot go."

Brightbill stomped around the garden and squawked, "This isn't fair!"

"I promise I will take you to see them when you are older," said the robot.

"But I want to go *now*!"

"Please calm down."

"You can't even fly! I could take off and you wouldn't be able to stop me!"

Roz stood, and her long shadow fell across her son. The gosling could feel his emotions swinging wildly. And for a moment he was actually afraid of his own mother. Without thinking, he sprinted toward the pond, beat his wings, and flew away.

CHAPTER 44

THE RUNAWAY

"Your son will be fine," said Loudwing. "You know how they are at this age."

"I do not know," said Roz. "Please tell me how they are at this age."

"Oh, right. Well, Brightbill is growing up fast. It's only natural for adolescent goslings to be a little...moody. He just needs to be alone for a while. You've raised a wonderful son. I know he'll come home soon. Try not to worry."

But Roz did worry. At least, she worried as much as a robot is capable of worrying. Brightbill had never run away—or flown away—and suddenly Roz was computing all the things that could go wrong. A violent storm. A broken wing. A predator. She had to find her son before something bad happened.

There was only one place Brightbill could have gone.

The robot gravesite. So Roz galloped northward. She leaped over rocks and ducked under branches and charged through meadows without ever slowing her pace. She raced all the way across the island until she finally stepped onto the sea cliffs above the gravesite.

And there was Brightbill. Perched on the edge, looking at the robot parts scattered on the shore below. His eyes were wet.

"Don't be angry!" he said as his mother walked over.

"I am not angry. But you should not have flown off

like that. You could have gotten hurt, or worse. I was worried sick!"

"I'm sorry, Mama."

"It is okay," said Roz. "It is only natural for goslings your age to be a little…moody."

"Mama, I need to understand what you are. And I think it might help to see those other robots."

"You are right—it might help. Why are you not down there?"

"I was about to go," said Brightbill, "but I got nervous. I want you to go with me."

"Let us go down there," said Roz. "Together."

CHAPTER 45
THE DEAD ROBOTS

The gosling floated on the breeze beside his mother as she climbed down the cliffside. Down they went, past ledges and seagulls and tough little trees, until they were standing on the rocky shore with the cliffs looming behind them.

The gravesite had changed. Roz's crate was gone, lost to weather or waves. Some of the robot parts were gone too. Other parts were gritty with sand, or were tangled in seaweed, or were inhabited by small, scuttling creatures. One smashed torso still had a head and legs attached. Roz and Brightbill huddled around the corpse and studied the mess of tubes spilling out.

"This thing used to look like you?" said Brightbill.

"Yes, we are the same type of robot," said Roz.

"And now this robot is dead?"

"In a way."

"Will you ever die, Mama?"

"I think so."

"Will I die?"

"All living things die eventually."

The gosling's face scrunched with worry.

"Brightbill, you are going to live a long and happy life!" Roz laid a hand on her son's back. "You should not worry about death."

The gosling's face relaxed. And then he pointed to a small, round shape on the back of the dead robot's head.

"What's that?" he said.

Roz leaned in closer. "That is a button, which is a knob on a piece of machinery that can be pressed to operate it."

Brightbill began pressing the button.

Click, click, click.

"Nothing is happening," he said. "Probably because this robot is dead."

Click, click, click.

"Mama, do you have a button?"

Brightbill watched as his mother's head turned all the way around and a small button came into view.

"You've got one!" he said. "I never noticed it before!"

"Neither did I," said the robot.

The gosling giggled. "Oh, Mama, you have so much to learn about yourself."

Roz reached for the button on her head, but her hand automatically stopped before she could touch it. She tried with her other hand, but it automatically stopped as well.

"It seems I cannot press the button," she said. "Would you like to try?"

"What will happen?"

"I think that I will shut down. But I think you could simply press the button again to restart me."

"You think?" squawked Brightbill. "What if you're wrong? What if you wake up different? What if you never wake up? Mama, I don't want to shut you down!"

Roz turned her head back around and saw that Brightbill's face was once again scrunched with worry. She knelt beside him and said, "Of course you do not have to shut me down! I am sorry if I scared you. Are you okay?"

"I'm okay." Brightbill sniffled and wiped his eyes. And then he heard splashing. Otters were playing in the ocean. He had never seen otters before. He stared as they swam and dove and sloshed around with one another. They seemed to be having a ridiculous amount of fun, and suddenly the gosling was smiling again.

"Hello, my name is Brightbill!" he shouted over the waves. "And this is my mama! Her name is Roz!"

The last time those otters had seen Roz, they had thought she was some kind of monster. But since then they'd heard that she was remarkably friendly and that she'd even adopted an orphaned gosling. And so the otters smiled at Roz and Brightbill. Then they swam straight over and splashed onto the rocks.

"Hello there!" said the biggest otter. "Nice to meet you

both! Actually, Roz, we've met once before, but you might not remember me. My name's Shelly."

"I do remember you," said the robot. "But I am glad to learn your name, Shelly."

"You know each other?" said the gosling.

"These otters were the first animals I ever met," said Roz. "They were also the first animals who ever ran away from me."

"Yeah, sorry about that," said Shelly as the other otters sniffed the robot's legs. "You know, Brightbill, when we first saw your mom, she was packed in a box and surrounded by soft squishy stuff..."

Brightbill's brow furrowed.

"You wouldn't believe how small she looked, all folded up in there..."

Brightbill's nose sniffled.

"We thought she was dead, but when we reached into the box, she came to life and climbed out looking like a sparkling monster!"

Brightbill's eyes welled up with tears, and then he felt his mother scoop him into her arms. "Are you okay?" she whispered in his ear.

"I think I've learned enough about robots for today," he whispered back.

"I am sorry, otters," said Roz, "but we really must be going."

"I hope I didn't upset the little guy!" said Shelly. "I thought he'd like to hear how we first met."

"Brightbill will be fine," said Roz, using a friendly voice. "But we have had a very busy day and we should go home. It was nice to see you again. Good-bye!"

Roz turned, and with her long strides, she carried her son away from the gravesite and over to the base of the sea cliffs.

"Would you like to sit on my shoulder as I climb?" said the robot.

"I feel like flying," said the gosling. "I'll meet you at the top."

Brightbill flapped his wings and disappeared into the sky. Roz began scaling the wall. Up she went, expertly negotiating rocky columns and ledges, until she hoisted herself onto the clifftop, where two young bears were waiting.

CHAPTER 46

THE FIGHT

"Hello, bears, my name is Roz."

"Oh, we know who you are," said the sister bear. Her voice dripped with sarcasm. "We're *very* happy to see you again."

"Yeah, we're *very* happy to see you again!" echoed the brother bear.

"Why do you always repeat what I say?" said the sister bear to her brother. "It's so annoying!"

"I was just backing you up!"

"Let me do the talking!"

"Fine! You don't have to be so mean about it!"

The bickering bears were interrupted by the robot's friendliest voice. "With whom do I have the pleasure of speaking?"

"How rude of us," said the sister bear. "My name is

139

Nettle, and this is my little brother, Thorn."

"I'm not little!" snapped Thorn under his breath.

"It is lovely to meet you both," said Roz. "But I am afraid I really must be going."

"And I'm afraid we can't let you do that." Nettle stepped into Roz's path. "My brother and I, we don't like monsters."

"I am not a monster. I am a robot."

"Whatever you are, we don't like you!" said Thorn.

"We hear you've become very comfortable on our island," said Nettle. "Now we're going to make you very *un*comfortable."

"Yeah, we're going to make you very *un*comfortable!"

"Stop repeating me, Thorn!"

Poor Roz was in serious trouble. The bears were closing in on her, but she couldn't run, she couldn't hide, and she couldn't fight. The robot didn't know what to do. But before she could do anything, there was a loud squawk and a streak of feathers.

"Stay away from my mama!" Brightbill swooped down and skidded to a stop between the robot and the bears.

"So the rumors are true!" Nettle laughed. "There really *is* a runty gosling who thinks the robot is his mother! How could anyone be so stupid! Do yourself a favor, gosling, and fly away before you get hurt!"

"She is right, Brightbill!" said Roz. "Please let me handle this!"

But the gosling stood his ground. He spread his wings and hopped around, ready to defend his mother. The bears roared with laughter. Then, with a flick of her paw, Nettle sent Brightbill tumbling over the ground, over and over, until he flopped onto his back and stared up at the sky, stunned.

"This is our island," snarled Nettle.

"And it's time for you to go," growled Thorn.

Roz made herself as big as possible. She banged her chest and roared wild, angry sounds. But the bears were not intimidated. They roared right back. And then they attacked.

Nettle pulled Roz into a fierce bear hug while Thorn clawed at her legs. The robot tried to shake free, but the bears would not let go of their prey, not this time. A cloud of dust bloomed around the trio as they thrashed closer to the edge of the cliff.

All of a sudden, something burst out from the trees and onto the open clifftop. Mother Bear. She was gigantic, like a mountain of golden fur. And she was furious. It seemed like this would be the end for our robot. But

Mother Bear wasn't there to join the fight. She was there to break it up. "Nettle! Thorn! *Get over here this instant!*"

The young bears should have listened to their mother. Instead they pretended not to hear her. Nettle slashed at Roz's body, and Thorn began wrestling with her foot. He grabbed the foot with both paws and forced it up from the ground. Then, with every ounce of his strength, he twisted the foot around.

Reader, the following events happened very quickly. First there was a strange *thwip* sound as the robot's right foot popped off her leg and sailed through the air. Then everyone toppled over. Nettle and Roz fell sideways along the edge. But Thorn fell backward and tumbled

right

off

the cliff.

Do you know what the most terrible sound in the world is? It's the howl of a mother bear as she watches her cub tumble off a cliff. Mother Bear's howl was so startling that it snapped Brightbill right out of his stupor. Her howl was so powerful that it shook Roz's entire body. Her howl was so loud that animals heard it clear across the island. But there was no reply from Thorn. Mother Bear's howl slowly faded, and she wilted to the ground.

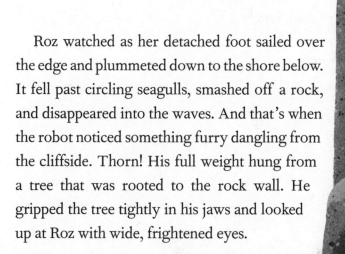

Roz watched as her detached foot sailed over the edge and plummeted down to the shore below. It fell past circling seagulls, smashed off a rock, and disappeared into the waves. And that's when the robot noticed something furry dangling from the cliffside. Thorn! His full weight hung from a tree that was rooted to the rock wall. He gripped the tree tightly in his jaws and looked up at Roz with wide, frightened eyes.

"I see Thorn!" shouted Roz. "Grab my legs! Quickly!"

Mother Bear and Nettle scrambled to their feet. Each bear took a leg in her mouth, and together they slowly lowered Roz headfirst down the cliff. Thorn whimpered through clenched teeth as he watched the robot approach. Then he felt her strong arms wrap around him and heard her booming voice holler, *"Pull us up!"*

Thorn let go of the branch and cried, "Please don't drop me, Roz! I don't want to die!"

"Do not worry," said the robot. "I will not drop you."

The next few moments seemed to drag on and on. Mother Bear and Nettle kept pulling on Roz's legs, and more of the robot slowly came into view until a furry golden head finally appeared, and Thorn leaped into the embrace of his family.

CHAPTER 47
THE PARADE

"Does it hurt?" Brightbill touched the smooth surface where his mother's foot used to be.

"No, it does not hurt," said Roz. "But it will be difficult for me to walk."

The bears huddled behind the gosling and stared at the robot's stump of a leg. Nobody understood how a foot could pop off like that, or how Roz could remain calm.

"Roz, I'm sorry my cubs attacked you," said Mother Bear. "Sometimes they're completely out of control."

"It is okay. You know how they are at this age."

"I can't thank you enough for saving Thorn. I promise my cubs will never bother you again. Isn't that right?"

"Yes, Mother," said Nettle and Thorn, together.

The robot tried to walk. She bobbed up and down on her uneven legs, which worked well enough on the flat surface of the clifftop, but once she entered the forest, her problem became clear. The smooth stump had no grip, and it slipped around on the forest floor. So Roz tried hopping on her one good foot. She took a few crunching hops and then clanged into a tree trunk. A few more hops and she crashed into the undergrowth.

"I'm really sorry I broke off your foot," said Thorn as he helped the robot up from the weeds.

"I forgive you," said Roz. Whether she was capable of true forgiveness is anybody's guess. But they were nice words, and Thorn felt better when he heard them.

"It looks like I will have to crawl home," said Roz.

"Nonsense!" said Mother Bear. "I have a better idea."

Mother Bear lay flat on the ground while her cubs boosted Roz onto her back. Then Brightbill fluttered onto the bear's broad shoulders. And when they were both safely aboard, the group set off through the forest.

The robot was heavy, but she was no trouble for the giant animal. Mother Bear strolled along as if it were perfectly normal for a robot to be riding on her back. They made quite a grand procession, all walking together like that. And the procession became even grander as deer and raccoons and birds and all kinds of other animals joined in. Everyone wanted to see the mother robot riding the mother bear. The group wound its way past ancient trees, and over rolling meadows, and through

babbling streams, collecting more and more curious animals as they went. It was the grandest parade of wildlife anyone had ever seen, and leading the way was our robot, Roz.

But the parade couldn't last forever. As the sun went down, the other animals began drifting away, one by one, and when the parade finally arrived at the Nest, only the original members remained.

"Here we are," said Mother Bear, helping Roz down into the garden. "Now, wasn't that better than crawling all the way home?"

"Oh, yes, that was wonderful!" said the robot. "I cannot imagine a better ending to this day. Thank you very much."

"Yeah, that was amazing!" squeaked the gosling. "My friends won't believe me when I tell them I rode across the island on the back of a bear!"

"I'm glad you enjoyed yourselves!" Mother Bear smiled. "It's the least I could do after all the trouble these two caused." Her smile became a frown, and she glared at her cubs, who suddenly took great interest in a pebble on the ground.

It was late, and it had been a long, difficult day for

everyone, so the bears said good-bye and headed back to their cave. Brightbill and Roz stood in the garden and watched their new friends lumber away. And then the gosling said, "Mama, do you think you'll ever walk again?"

"I am not sure," said the robot, "but I know who to ask for help. Now go get ready for bed."

CHAPTER 48

THE NEW FOOT

Mr. Beaver squinted at Roz's stump.

"I've never built a foot before." He stroked his whiskers and muttered to himself. "There are really three problems to solve. The foot needs to grip the ground. And it needs to be durable. And then there's the issue of fixing it to the leg. I might have to consult a few friends."

"Will she ever walk again?" said Brightbill.

"What's that?" Mr. Beaver was lost in thought. "Oh, not to worry. You just sit back and leave everything to me. I love a challenge!"

Mr. Beaver plunked into the pond, and returned a while later rolling a large section of a tree trunk. "Say hello to your new foot!" he said, slapping the wood with his tail.

"Hello, new foot," said the robot.

"That's the spirit! This beauty is from one of the hardest trees I ever chewed. I just need to make a few modifications."

Mr. Beaver placed the piece of wood next to Roz. He squinted, repositioned the piece, and squinted some more. With his claws, he marked different spots on the wood. And then he put his big chompers to work. The beaver chewed and gnawed and carved up that piece of wood, turning it over and over in his paws.

Chitchat looked down from a branch and chattered through the quiet moments. "This reminds me of the time I saw a fox catch a lizard by the tail and somehow the lizard's tail fell off and he got away and later I saw that the lizard got a new tail and now Roz is going to get a new foot and everything will be fine..."

The wooden foot took shape, and before long Mr. Beaver was standing beside a beautiful carving that resembled a boot. He tried to slide it over Roz's stump, but the opening was too small. So he scraped out more wood until it was a perfect fit.

"Very good," he said, spitting out a wood chip. "My friends should be arriving any minute with the next few things we'll need. And there they are now! I'd like you all to meet Bumpkin, Lumpkin, and Rumpkin. But I call them the Fuzzy Bandits."

Three fat raccoons shuffled into the garden, dragging a tangle of vines behind them.

"Good day," said Bumpkin.

"Good day," said Lumpkin.

"Good day," said Rumpkin.

You might already know this, reader, but raccoons have very nimble hands. And the Fuzzy Bandits used theirs to skillfully tie those vines around the robot's leg and around her new foot. The vines caught nicely on all the dings and dents and scrapes. Once they were tied good and tight, Mr. Beaver threw back his head and hollered, "Trunktap! We could use your assistance!"

There was silence.

And then three quick taps echoed down from the forest canopy.

"Ah, that'll be him," said Mr. Beaver, smiling.

A very handsome woodpecker swooped into the garden. "You called?" came the woodpecker's musical voice.

"Indeed I did! Everyone, this is my wood-pecking pal, Trunktap. Now, Trunky, we need some tree resin, the really sticky stuff. Can you help us out?"

"Of course I can!" said the woodpecker. "You've got a perfect pine right here!"

Trunktap hopped over to a crusty old pine tree and pecked a few deep holes in the bark. Thick, syrupy resin began oozing down the trunk. Mr. Beaver scooped up handfuls of the resin and smeared it all over the wooden foot and the vines until everything was glistening with stickiness. And when the resin dried a short time later, Roz's foot was finished.

"This is wonderful!" said the robot as she strolled around her garden. "I am as good as new!"

Mr. Beaver and Trunktap and the Fuzzy Bandits went away feeling pretty happy with themselves. They'd done a very nice thing. But it was the first wooden foot any of them had ever made. And within a week the vines were coming undone and the foot was sliding loose. So they returned, determined to get it right. They found even harder wood and even tougher vines. They experimented with resin, heating it by the fire, letting it boil and thicken, until it became an indestructible glue. They kept tinkering with their design until, finally, Roz had herself a wooden foot that she could rely on.

"Huzzah!" Mr. Beaver rapped his knuckles on the new-and-improved creation. "I knew we'd get it right."

Roz moved slower than before, and she had a slight limp, but she was back to her old self again, and that was a relief to everyone, especially Brightbill.

CHAPTER 49
THE FLIER

With coaching from his mother, Brightbill was becoming a truly exceptional flier. He wasn't the biggest or the strongest, but he was the smartest. You see, he and his mother had started studying the flying techniques of other birds. They'd sit for hours and watch how hawks and owls and sparrows and vultures moved through the air. Then they'd go up to the grassy ridge and Brightbill would practice what he'd learned. Soon, he was diving and swooping and darting and soaring around the island. The adult geese frowned at his flying tricks, but the goslings thought he was amazing.

Each morning, a gaggle of them would wait on the water for Brightbill to lead them into the sky. And then a few hours later he'd return home to Roz, shaking his tail feathers and honking about his latest airborne adventures.

"Mama! The other goslings didn't know that warm air rises. So I found an updraft and we spent the afternoon circling around and around and hardly flapped our wings at all!"

"Mama! Did you see that lightning storm today? We knew there was trouble when the wind started blowing from the north, so we flew down to some shrubs and waited for the storm to pass."

"Mama! We just tried to fly in formation! We all took turns at the point, but everyone liked following me the best, so I led most of the time."

CHAPTER 50

THE BUTTON

Brightbill was thinking about the small button on the back of his mother's head. His mother was thinking about it too. They couldn't stop wondering what would happen if the button were pressed. And one day, they decided it was time to find out.

Roz sat on the floor of the Nest. Her son nervously stood on a stone behind her.

"I am ready when you are," said the robot.

"Okay," said the gosling. "Here we go."

Brightbill took a deep breath.

Click.

Roz's body relaxed.

Her quiet whirring slowly stopped.

Her eyes faded to black.

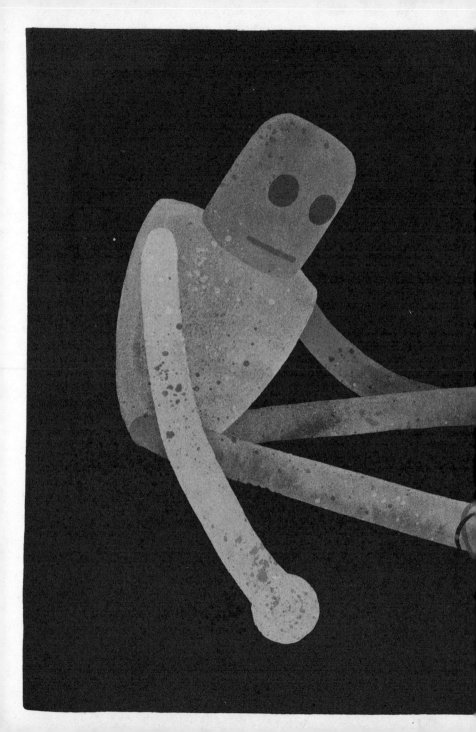

"Mama, can you hear me?"

There was no answer. Brightbill waddled around and looked at his mother's face. Her strange spark of life had gone out. The gosling had never felt more alone.

He was ready to switch her back on. But what if she didn't wake up? What if she woke up different? The gosling was afraid to press the button, and he was afraid not to press the button.

Brightbill took a deep breath.

Click.

Roz's body tensed.

Her quiet whirring slowly started.

Her eyes began to glow.

"Mama, can you hear me?"

"Hello, I am ROZZUM unit 7134, but you may call me Roz." The robot spoke these words automatically, in a language Brightbill didn't understand. His little heart raced as his worst fears seemed to be coming true. But a moment later, her familiar voice returned, and the robot said in the language of the animals, "Hello, son. How long was I out? It seemed like only an instant to me."

"You were out for a few minutes," said the gosling as he hugged his mother. "But it seemed like forever to me."

THE AUTUMN

The days were getting shorter. The air was getting crisper. And one morning, Roz walked out to find a layer of frost on the garden. Autumn had come to the island.

The tree leaves, which had been green for the robot's entire life, turned yellow and orange and red. Then they let go of their branches and floated down to the ground, and the forest gradually filled with the sounds of creatures scurrying through dead leaves. Tree nuts were also falling, thunking onto roots and rocks and occasionally clanging off the robot. The smell of flowers faded as blossoms withered. All the rich scents and colors of the island were draining away.

The animals were also changing. Furry animals

were growing more fur. Feathery animals were growing more feathers. Scaly animals were starting to look for new homes.

"Yurp. It's cooling off," croaked one frog to another. "Before long it'll be time for sleeping."

"Yurp. I'd better start looking for a good hole," croaked the second frog. "Have you found one yet?"

"Nah," croaked the first frog. "I'll look for a hole next week. For now, I'm going to enjoy the warm sunlight while it lasts. Yurp."

Many of the island animals were already thinking about their winter hibernation. Frogs, bees, snakes, and even bears would soon disappear and spend the next few months resting out of sight.

And then there were the birds. Some birds, like owls and woodpeckers, would spend the winter nesting and eating the island's few remaining edibles. But the migratory birds were preparing for the long journey south to their warm wintering grounds. And among the birds destined to leave were the geese.

CHAPTER 52

THE FLOCK

Brightbill slowly waddled into the Nest. He had a confused look on his face.

"Mama? The other goslings said that we have to leave the island soon, and we won't return for months and months. Is that true?"

"That is true," said Roz. "You know that geese migrate south for the winter."

"Will you migrate with us?" said Brightbill.

"I cannot fly or swim, so I will spend the winter here on the island."

"Can I stay with you?"

"I do not think that is a good idea. I think you should migrate with the flock."

"How long will the migration take?" said Brightbill. "Where will we fly? When will we come home?"

"I do not know," said Roz. "Let us go ask the others."

And so the robot and the gosling walked around the pond, to where Loudwing and her friends were chatting. "Hello, everyone," said Roz. "Brightbill has some questions about the flock's upcoming winter migration."

"And we'd be happy to answer them!" said Loudwing. "What would you like to know, little one?"

"How long will the migration take?" said Brightbill. "Where will we fly? When will we come home?"

"It'll take us a couple of weeks to fly south," said Loudwing, "depending on the weather."

"We'll join other flocks at a beautiful lake in the middle of a great, sprawling field," said another goose.

"And we'll come back to the island after four or five months," said someone else, "depending on the weather."

As they walked back to the Nest, Brightbill said to his mother, "Lately I've been feeling this strong urge to fly. Not just around the pond or the island, but to go on a long flight. A journey."

"Those are your instincts," said the robot. "All animals have instincts. They help you survive."

"Do you have instincts?" said the gosling.

"I do have instincts. They help me survive also."

"My instincts are definitely telling me to fly south for the winter," said Brightbill. "I just wish you could join us. I'm going to worry about you while I'm away."

"Do not worry. I will be fine," said Roz. "How bad could winter be?"

CHAPTER 53

THE MIGRATION

It was the night before the migration, and Brightbill was sleeping fitfully. Roz watched him toss and turn until he finally crawled up into her arms, and she rocked him to sleep, just like the old days.

Early the next morning, Brightbill waddled outside and looked at the pond. The water was perfectly still. A few lazy clouds drifted above. Geese were already gathering by the beach. And then tiny claws scampered down from the treetops.

"So today's the day huh?" said Chitchat, perched on a branch. "You're going to see so many new things and meet so many new animals and if there are any squirrels at your wintering grounds please tell them that Chitchat says hello!"

"Today is the day," said Brightbill. "The flock will be leaving soon."

"Are you excited or nervous or scared?"

"I'm all of those things."

The squirrel whispered, "Well don't worry about your mother I'll look after her so you know she'll be perfectly fine."

Brightbill smiled.

"I am afraid it is time to go," said Roz as she stepped out of the Nest.

"Okay, Mama," said the gosling. "See you in the spring, Chitchat!"

"Have a nice migration Brightbill!" The squirrel scampered back into the treetops. "Come home with lots of exciting stories but not too exciting because I don't want anything scary to happen to you good-bye!"

The geese were honking with excitement and hustling around as they made their final preparations. Several of the fathers huddled together, discussing their flight plans, while the mothers took a head count.

"There you are, Brightbill!" Loudwing honked from the middle of the crowd. "We're just about to begin!"

"May I have your attention, please!" said the biggest goose. "As most of you know, my name is Longneck, and

I'll be leading this year's migration. I'm asking everyone to please join your families for takeoff. Once we're all airborne, each family will take its position in our V formation, and we'll start the first leg of our journey. Are there any questions?"

"I have a question," came a booming voice. "My son will not have any family with him. Where does he fit into the formation?"

Everyone turned to Longneck.

"He can fly with me," said the big goose. "I hear Brightbill is a very clever flier—I could use his help at the point."

A moment later, the geese began flapping and honking and making their way into the air. A cloud of feathers floated down around the robot and her son.

"You are not a gosling anymore," said Roz. "I am proud of the fine young goose you have become."

Brightbill fluttered up to his mother's shoulder.

"Thanks, Mama." The young goose wiped his eyes. "Is this where we say good-bye?"

"This is where we say good-bye for now. Spring will soon be here, and we will be together again."

"I'm going to miss you," said Brightbill as he nuzzled his mother.

"I am going to miss you too," said Roz as she nuzzled her son.

The goose took a deep breath. Then he shook his tail feathers, flapped his wings, and joined the flock.

At first, the geese flew in a disorganized jumble. But each goose slowly drifted into position until the flock formed a wobbly V. At the lead was Longneck, and behind his left wing was Brightbill. They circled in the sky until the V pointed south, and then the geese began their long migration. Roz climbed to the top of a tree and watched as the flock slowly faded into the horizon.

CHAPTER 54
THE WINTER

The island was quiet. The migratory birds had all left, the hibernators were asleep, and everyone else had begun their simple winter routines. Everyone but Roz. Now that she was alone, our robot didn't know what to do with herself. She stood in her gray garden and watched a sheet of ice slowly form on the pond. Sometimes she could hear her good friends the beavers going about their business beneath the ice, and she wondered when she would see them again.

Roz stood there until snowflakes started drifting down from the sky. The flakes swirled in the breeze and slowly piled up on the ground and on the trees and on the robot. So she crouched into the Nest, slid the stone door behind her, and sat in darkness.

Hours, and days, and weeks went by without the robot

moving. She had no need to move; she felt perfectly safe in the Nest. And so, in her own way, the robot hibernated.

Roz's body relaxed.

Her quiet whirring slowly stopped.

Her eyes faded to black.

She probably could have spent centuries like that, hibernating in total darkness. But the robot's hibernation was suddenly interrupted when a shaft of sunlight fell upon her face and carried energy back to her empty battery.

Roz's body tensed.

Her quiet whirring slowly started.

Her eyes began to glow.

"Hello, I am ROZZUM unit 7134, but you may call me Roz," the robot said automatically.

When all her systems were up and running again, Roz noticed that she was surrounded by broken branches and piles of snow. The roof of the Nest had caved in, and the lodge was now flooded with sunlight. Roz felt more energized with each passing minute. But she also felt cold. Her joints felt stiff and brittle, and her thinking was slow. So she got up, cleared a spot on the floor, and made a fire. The snow inside the Nest began to melt and the robot's sensors began to thaw, and when she was ready,

she climbed out through the hole in the roof and into a bright, foreign landscape.

The world Roz had known was now covered in a thick layer of snow. Tree limbs bent to the ground under heavy sleeves. The dark pond was now pure white. The only sounds were Roz's own crunching footsteps.

Faint wisps of steam curled up from the robot's body as she trudged through the forest. Roz plunged a hand into a lump of snow and pulled up a long stick. She snapped it in half and flung both pieces back to the Nest. She took a few more steps and picked up a fallen tree. She hacked it into smaller pieces and flung them back as well.

Then she reached down to another snowy shape. But what she pulled up was not a piece of wood. It was Dart the weasel. He was frozen solid. Roz stared at his stiff body for a moment, then decided it was best to leave the poor thing where he was.

As the robot continued gathering wood, she found more victims of the cold. A frozen mouse. A frozen bird. A frozen deer. Had all the island animals frozen to death? No, not all. There were a few fresh tracks in the snow.

As we know, the wilderness is filled with beauty, but it's also filled with ugliness. And that winter was ugly. A devastating cold front had swept down from the north and brought dangerous temperatures and huge amounts of snow. The animals had prepared for winter. But nothing could have prepared the weaker ones for those long nights, when the temperature plummeted and the wind whipped over the island.

Roz returned to the Nest, where the fire had melted the interior snow to a muddy soup. She took a minute to warm her body by the flames, and then she began the repairs. She patched up the hole in the dome with a latticework of branches before adding a layer of mud and leaves, and soon the repairs were complete. But another snowfall might cave in the Nest all over again. So Roz decided to keep a fire going day and night to prevent snow from building up on the roof.

The robot brought in load after load of firewood. And each time she went outside, she was reminded of the frozen weasel and mouse and bird and deer. How many other frozen animals were hidden beneath the snow?

Before going in for the night, she called out to whoever was listening.

"Animals of the island! You do not have to freeze! Join me in my lodge, where it is safe and warm!"

CHAPTER 55
THE LODGERS

Firelight spilled out from the Nest and into the cold, blustery night. Roz sat inside and listened to the wind and to the soft pops and crackles of burning wood. And then the robot's keen hearing picked up another sound: tiny footsteps crunching through snow.

"Roz I'm freezing can I join you by the fire please?" said a weak voice.

Into the light crawled Chitchat. The squirrel was shivering, and clumps of ice stuck to her fur. When she finally felt the heat of the fire, she collapsed. Roz picked her up off the floor, gently placed her on a warm stone, and let her sleep.

An hour later, there were more footsteps, and a family of hares shuffled into the Nest. They huddled together in a corner without saying a word. Pinktail the opossum

was the next to arrive. "Good evening," she mumbled,
trying to act cheerful. "It certainly has been ch-ch-chilly."
Swooper the owl hobbled in, followed by some chickadees
and a magpie. Fink knew a good thing when he saw it, and
the fox lay down right by the fire. Then came Digdown
the groundhog. The Fuzzy Bandits carried in an old turtle
named Crag, who was in the worst shape of all. Creatures
who should have been hibernating deep underground had
been roused by that vicious weather. Only the healthiest
animals with the warmest homes were safe. More and more

weary animals appeared, and slowly the lodge filled up.

This was the first time many of the lodgers had seen fire, and they gazed at it with a mixture of fear and hope. They could feel the fire's destructive power, but they could also feel its healing power as it warmed their bones. The lodgers seemed to push forward, eager to feel more warmth, and then pull back, afraid of feeling too much.

It was important that the lodgers understood fire. So Roz showed them how to build one. She showed the smaller animals how to arrange the kindling, and she showed the bigger animals how to arrange the logs. Bumpkin, Lumpkin, and Rumpkin struck the firestones together, and everyone cheered when they finally managed a spark.

As Roz looked around, she saw moles curling up beside an owl. A mouse snuggling between two weasels. Hares nestling against a badger. Never before had the robot seen prey and predators so close and peaceful. But how long could the peace possibly last?

"I propose a truce," said Roz, "like the Dawn Truce. Everyone must agree not to hunt or harm one another while in my lodge."

"Very well," said Swooper, after consulting his carnivorous friends. "We hunters will control ourselves."

"Then it is settled," said Roz. "My home is a safe place for all."

One by one, the lodgers each fell into a deep sleep. Even the nocturnal creatures, usually wide awake at that hour, gave in to the coziness of the Nest. The robot stood out of the way and quietly tended to the fire as her guests slept through the night. Only when daylight was streaming in through the door did the lodgers finally begin to stir.

"You are all welcome to stay here as long as you like," said the robot as the animals rubbed sleep from their eyes. "My home is your home."

"Thanks a lot, Roz." Fink carefully stepped over a hare and a woodpecker on his way to the door. "I don't think I would have survived another night on my own. It's just too bad we can't cram a few more creatures in here." And the fox slipped outside.

The robot looked down at the fur and feathers that now carpeted the floor. The Nest had been completely full that night. If any more animals showed up, they'd be left out in the cold. But Roz was not about to let that happen.

CHAPTER 56

THE NEW LODGES

The second lodge would have to be bigger than the first if it was going to fit Broadfoot the bull moose. He was a towering hulk of an animal and had a thick coat of fur, but even he was struggling with the frigid temperatures.

Broadfoot lived on the other side of the pond, in a dense section of forest that was home to many animals, most of whom were in desperate need of a good thaw. The winter days were short, so there was no time to waste, and rather than walking all the way around the pond, Roz tested its frozen surface to see if it was safe to cross. She threw a heavy rock high in the air and watched it bounce off the hard ice. Then she carefully walked over the ice and into the forest on the other side, where she found Broadfoot waiting for her. The moose quietly led the robot to the clearing in the trees where the new lodge would go. Then Roz made a fire and watched as cold creatures began crawling out from the shadows.

"Do not worry," the robot said to the growing crowd, steam puffing from their noses. "You will all be warm soon. But I need your help."

Roz asked the animals to collect anything useful they could find: large stones, strong branches, chunks of frozen mud. With the robot's building expertise, and the small army of helpers, construction of the second lodge didn't take long. The animals happily agreed to the robot's truce, and then they shuffled into the warm wooden dome. "If you keep the fire alive, it will keep you alive," explained Roz as she dropped another log onto the flames. "But be careful. Fire can turn deadly in an instant."

At dawn, heavy snow was falling again, and there was Roz, setting out from the Nest to build a third lodge. She trudged into the Great Meadow, where fierce winds had created enormous, sweeping snow-drifts. But she powered through and finished the job, and was soon beginning work on a fourth lodge. And then a fifth.

The island became dotted with lodges that all glowed warmly through those long winter nights. And inside each one, animals laughed and shared stories and cheered their good friend Roz.

CHAPTER 57

THE FIRE

Strange sounds were echoing from the far side of the pond. What started as a low murmur gradually swelled to a chorus of terrified voices. There was an eerie glow in that part of the forest, and a thick plume of smoke began rising up from the snowy treetops.

Roz charged across the ice and found the second lodge completely engulfed by a raging fire. Frightened animals were running in every direction, fleeing for their lives through the deep snow.

"What happened?" shouted Roz as Broadfoot galloped wildly past.

"We put too many logs in the fire pit!" he said without stopping. "The flames climbed up to the ceiling!"

"My baby is still in there!" cried a

mother hare, pointing at the burning lodge. "Somebody help! Please!"

Roz didn't hesitate. She plowed through the snow and ducked into the lodge. Flames and smoke were everywhere. A tall stack of logs blazed in the fire pit. And in the far corner, a tiny ball of fur was shaking with fear. Crouching low, the robot wound her way beneath the smoke and around the flames and gently scooped up the young hare.

"Do not worry!" Roz yelled over the roar of the fire. "You are going to be okay!"

She turned to leave, but the doorway had started to crumble. So she shielded the hare with her body and smashed right through the walls of the lodge. Sizzling pieces of wood went flying as the robot and the hare burst outside into the soft snow.

"Oh, darling, you're all right!" cried the mother hare, pulling her daughter close. "Thank you for saving my baby, Roz!"

Now that everyone was safely away, the robot turned her attention to putting out the fire. Her glowing eyes darted around as she computed a plan. Then, with all the strength in her legs, Roz launched herself high up into the snowy branches of the nearest pine tree. A moment later, the tree was shaking violently and heaps of snow were sliding from its branches and pouring onto the flames like an avalanche. Steam hissed up through the smothering mound of snow. The flames quickly died, the snow quickly melted, and within minutes all that remained was the charred foundation of the lodge.

Roz dropped down from the tree and waited as the frightened animals slowly returned. Then she said to them, "Would you like another lodge?"

The animals looked at one another, unsure of what to do. Understandably, they were afraid of another fire breaking out. But they were far more afraid of the deadly cold. So they pulled together and worked with Roz and built a bigger, better lodge on top of the old one. It had a taller ceiling and a deeper fire pit, it was made with more rock and less wood, and it had a supply of water for emergencies. But the most important safety features of this rebuilt lodge were the lodgers themselves, who now had a whole new respect for fire.

CHAPTER 58

THE CONVERSATIONS

Thanks to Roz's truce, life inside the Nest was mostly harmonious. But when the animals went outside, it was business as usual. Sometimes a lodger wouldn't return. Sometimes a lodger would return in the belly of another lodger. As you can imagine, that made for some awkward moments. So when everyone was gathered around the fire, they tried to keep things pleasant by having conversations like these.

"I wonder what Brightbill is doing right now." Chitchat lay on her back and looked at the ceiling as she spoke. "And where he is and who he's with and if he ever thinks about us back here on the island."

"I am sure he thinks about us," said Roz. "I think about him all the time."

"I like to imagine that the geese had a fun flight to the wintering grounds and now Brightbill is floating on a lovely lake eating yummy food and making wonderful new friends but hopefully they're not too wonderful because I'd like to stay his best friend if possible."

"That is a nice thought," said Roz. "But I worry that the flock might have gotten caught in this icy weather. I do not think they would handle it well."

"Don't worry I'm sure they're fine," said Chitchat. "Brightbill is such a great flier that I just know he'll keep the flock out of trouble."

"He is a great flier," said Roz. "But I still worry."

"Life is short." Digdown the old groundhog was giving another one of her fireside speeches. "I'll be lucky if I see the spring. I don't want your pity. I've had a good run. But I'll tell you what: If I could do it all over again, I'd spend more time helping others. All I've ever done is dig tunnels. Some of them were real beauties too, but they're all hidden underground, where they're no good to anyone but me. And they weren't even good to me this winter! Now, the beavers, they have it all figured out. They built that beautiful dam, which created a lovely pond that made all our lives better. That must feel mighty good!"

"The beavers made our lives better in another way," said Fink. "They taught Roz how to build."

"Ain't that the truth!" said Digdown. "Roz, you must have saved half the island with your lodges! And to think we used to call you a monster. I'll repay my debt to you if it's the last thing I do."

"Your friendship is payment enough," said Roz.

"Oh, please, your sweetness is gonna make me sick. There must be something we can do!"

"Your friendship really is enough. Friends help each other. And I will need all the help I can get. My mind is strong, but my body will not last forever. I want to survive as long as possible. And to do that I will need the help of my friends."

The animals listened quietly to Roz and thought of their own struggles to survive. Life in the wilderness was hard for everyone; there was no escaping that fact. But the robot had made their lives a little easier. And if ever they could, the animals would return the favor.

"I have seen ninety-three winters, far more than any of you." Crag the turtle spoke slowly, but everyone always listened to his words. "And I can tell you that the winters have gotten colder, and the summers have gotten hotter, and the storms have gotten fiercer."

"I heard that the ocean has gotten higher," said Chitchat, "but I don't see how that could be true I mean where would all that extra water come from?"

"You are right—the ocean is higher," said Crag. "My grandfather used to say that, long ago, this island was not an island at all. It was a mountain surrounded by flatlands. And then the ground shook, and the oceans grew, and the land slowly flooded until the mountain became this island. Animals from far and wide were forced to come here to escape the floodwaters. In those early days, there were too many animals living in too small a place. The island did not have enough food to feed them all. But between fighting and disease and famine, a balance was finally reached. And we have kept the balance ever since."

Chitchat's eyes grew wide with concern. "If the ocean

keeps rising the island will be swallowed up by the waves and I don't even know how to swim!"

"If the waves ever do swallow this island, it will not happen for a very long time," said Crag. "By then we will all be long dead, even me."

"Everything has a purpose." It was Swooper's turn to lecture the lodgers. "The sun is meant to give light. Plants are meant to grow. We owls are meant to hunt."

"We mice are meant to hide."

"We raccoons are meant to scavenge."

"Roz, what are you meant to do?"

"I do not believe I have a purpose."

"Ha! I respectfully disagree," said Swooper. "Clearly, you are meant to build."

"I think Roz is meant to grow gardens."

"Roz is definitely meant to care for Brightbill."

"Perhaps I am simply meant to help others."

CHAPTER 59
THE SPRING

Dripping water, flowing water, splashing water. Winter's blanket of snow and ice was finally beginning to melt. White was fading away to expose the grays and browns that had been hidden beneath. Little green buds were appearing all over. Crowds of bright flowers were rising up from the dirt. And soon the island would be bursting with rich scents and colors. At long last it was spring.

The lodgers returned to their own homes. The hibernators emerged from their secret places. Roz roamed across the island and checked in with the beavers and the bears and all the friends she'd missed. Then the robot went home to work in her garden. After the bitterest winter anyone could recall, life was slowly returning to normal.

However, it was a quiet spring. There were fewer insects buzzing, fewer birds singing, fewer rodents rustling. Many creatures had frozen to death over the winter. And as the last of the snow melted away, their corpses were slowly revealed. The wilderness really can be ugly sometimes. But from that ugliness came beauty. You see, those poor dead creatures returned to the earth, their bodies nourished the soil, and they helped create the most dazzling spring bloom the island had ever known.

CHAPTER 60

THE FISH

"Help! Help! He's got my tail!" Paddler was splashing and screaming in the pond. Mr. and Mrs. Beaver were nowhere to be seen, so Roz picked up a fallen tree branch and stomped into the shallows.

"Grab on to this!" she said as she reached out with the branch. Paddler grabbed it with his big teeth, and the robot lifted him up out of the water. And there, hanging from the young beaver's tail, was Rockmouth, the grumpy old pike. In one quick movement, Roz pulled in the branch and gripped the fish with her two hands. Paddler flopped into the water, where his parents suddenly appeared.

"What is wrong with you, Rockmouth?" Mrs. Beaver dragged her son away. "You've always been a nuisance, but this time you've gone too far! Do us all a favor, Roz, and toss him to the vultures!"

"I cannot do that," said the robot. "But I might be able to help."

Roz placed Rockmouth in a deep puddle near the pond where he couldn't swim away. Then she waited for the fish to explain himself. Fish aren't very talkative, especially grumpy fish like Rockmouth. But eventually he opened up to the robot, and before long she was waving for the beavers to join them.

"Rockmouth used to live in the river," said Roz as the beavers shuffled over. "But you trapped him here when you built your dam. He has been angry about it ever since."

"That doesn't give him the right to attack my son!" hollered Mr. Beaver.

"It most certainly does not!" hollered Mrs. Beaver.

"I'd be upset too," said Paddler softly. "I'd hate to be kept away from my home. Mr. Rockmouth, you should have said something sooner!"

The fish looked up from the puddle with a frustrated expression that meant "I tried, but no one was listening."

Well, the situation had to be remedied. And you can guess who rose to the occasion. Roz was determined to get Rockmouth back to his home. After she explored the nearby waterways, it became clear that she would have to carry the pike through the forest and across the Great Meadow to the nearest bend in the river.

"I need a large container," said Roz to the beavers. "Something I can fill with water so Rockmouth can breathe while I carry him home. I could make it myself, but I thought you might like to help."

It couldn't have been easy to overcome her anger with Rockmouth, but after Mrs. Beaver had a chance to cool off, she finally came around. "I suppose we're partly to blame for this whole situation," she muttered. Then the beavers did the right thing, and together they carved out a wooden barrel for the fish.

"Here you go." Mrs. Beaver rolled the barrel over to the puddle, where the robot and the fish were waiting. "This should work nicely. Rockmouth, I hope you're happy back in the river."

Rockmouth just flicked his tail in a way that meant "Will someone please take me home now!"

Roz filled the barrel with water and a grumpy fish, and then they were off. She carried Rockmouth through the forest and across the meadow until she was standing on the riverbank.

"Welcome home," said the robot. Then she tipped the barrel and the fish plunked into the river. Rockmouth's face poked above the surface, he flashed a big toothy grin, and then he quickly swam away.

CHAPTER 61
THE ROBOT STORIES

The story of how Roz helped Rockmouth spread through the river and across the island. And it was soon followed by other robot stories. There were stories of Roz growing gardens in dry, barren places. There were stories of Roz nursing sick animals back to health. There were stories of Roz creating ropes and wheels and tools for helping her friends. But most of the new stories were about the robot's wildness.

You see, Roz had noticed that the wilder she acted, the more the animals liked her. And so she barked with foxes and sang with birds and hissed with snakes. She romped with weasels. She sunbathed with lizards. She leaped with deer. That spring was a very wild time for our robot.

CHAPTER 62

THE RETURN

It was a quiet afternoon on the pond. But the quiet was gradually being overtaken by sounds not heard around there for many months. The sounds grew louder and louder, and then a flock of geese appeared above the trees.

Honk! Honk! Honk!

Most flocks of geese move lazily through the sky and trail off in wobbly lines. But not this one. This flock was fast. It flew in a perfect V formation. And it was led by a small, graceful goose.

The flock flew once around the pond before gliding down and gently splashing into the water. The geese gathered in a tight group in the middle of the pond. They floated there for a while, softly honking to one another.

And then the leader broke away from the others. He swam straight toward the Nest, waddled into the garden, and fluttered up to his mother's shoulder.

"Welcome home, son," said Roz.

"It's good to be back, Ma," said Brightbill.

CHAPTER 63
THE JOURNEY

After months of separation, Roz and Brightbill, mother and son, were together again. And they had so much catching up to do. They went into the Nest, and the robot built a fire. Then the goose gazed into the flames and told the story of his winter. This is what he said.

"We spent the whole first day of our migration flying over the ocean. It seemed like the ocean would go on forever, but just when the flock was getting tired, Longneck pointed to some tiny islands on the horizon. We flew down to one of the islands and ate dune grass and rested our wings. After a few days of hopping from island to island, we reached the mainland and continued over fields and forests. And then the snow began to fall.

"I'd never seen snow before, and at first I thought it was beautiful! But it just kept coming. The others explained that the snow was early, that we were never supposed to see it, but there it was, piling up around us as we tried to sleep at night. Longneck worried that the weakest geese wouldn't survive, and he was right. We lost old Widefoot to that very first snowstorm.

"We tried to fly around the snowy weather, but we got completely lost and the weather became even worse. Lakes and ponds and rivers began freezing over. We couldn't find food or water, so we ate snow, and that only made us colder. We had trouble cleaning ourselves, and our feathers became dirty and heavy. The flock was in bad shape. But Longneck kept us moving. 'We are geese,' he squawked, 'and geese keep going!'

"One day, we were struggling through a snow shower when we saw something called a farm. It had perfectly square fields and enormous buildings. And stomping her way through the farm was a robot! She looked just like you, Ma!

"Longneck sent me over to speak to the robot, but I couldn't understand anything she said, so I just followed her through the farm and around a corner, and then I saw something I never expected.

"Plants! Bright, colorful plants! I didn't understand how plants could live in such cold weather, but then I saw that they were actually inside a building. I learned later that the building was called a greenhouse, and it had clear walls made of something called glass. The robot pressed a button on the wall, and a door slid open and warm air came rushing out. I hadn't felt warmth in so long that I just had to follow her inside.

"Ma, it was like summer in there! The air was warm and sweet and sticky. And there were rows and rows of different plants. The robot didn't pay any attention to me, so I wandered around the greenhouse, nibbling on leaves and drinking from puddles. Then I heard a scratchy voice behind me.

"'If I were younger, I woulda killed you by now.'

"I spun around, and there was an old cat! She walked on stiff legs, and her fur was gray and clumpy. The cat's name was Snooks, and she didn't seem very nice. But then she saw the other geese out in the cold with their faces pressed against the glass, and she told me how to open the door.

"'You can rest here,' said Snooks as the flock hurried in. 'But stay outta sight! The humans aren't as friendly as me.'

"None of us knew what 'humans' were, but we didn't care. We were just happy to be out of the cold. Loudwing was so happy she cried. The flock drank and ate and bathed and slept and stayed out of the way. Snooks showed us where to leave our droppings so they wouldn't be noticed. And for a few days, the greenhouse was our home.

"Once or twice a day, the robot would go outside and return with a box or a bag, but most of the time she stayed inside and quietly worked on the plants.

"There was a barn that I just had to explore. It was filled with animals and

machines and piles of straw, and two robots. One robot was fixing a broken door when I walked in. She was using a loud spinning tool called a saw. She pushed the saw through a long piece of wood, and dust shot into the air. Everything was going smoothly until the saw suddenly lurched forward and sliced right through three of the robot's fingers! But she was fine. A minute later there was a *thwip* sound as she popped on a new hand. Then she went right back to using the saw again! The other robot worked with the animals. Chickens, sheep, pigs, and cows. They were all in cages. The chickens kept asking me how I'd gotten out of my cage. I was explaining that I'd never had a cage when I heard panicked squawks coming from the greenhouse.

"I ran back and found that a human had discovered the flock. We didn't know what he was saying, but he looked really angry. Longneck tried to defend us. He got in front and spread his wings and honked, but the human wasn't afraid. He pulled out a shiny stick and pointed it right at Longneck. Snooks hissed, 'Look out, he's got a rifle!' Suddenly, a bright beam of light shot out from the rifle, and Longneck slumped to the floor. He was dead, Ma!

"The flock was so scared. We fluttered around and honked and knocked over plants. But the human kept moving toward us, pointing his rifle. So I pecked the button to open the door, and we ran outside, into the cold, and flew away from there as fast as we could.

"Without Longneck, the flock needed a new leader. Everyone wanted me to lead. I didn't know what to do, so I started by repeating Longneck's words. I squawked, 'We are geese, and geese keep going!' Then I took the point, and the flock spread out behind me.

"The weather had us all turned around, and nobody knew which way to go, so I just led us straight south. We saw more robots and humans and buildings, but we didn't stop. We knew we were way off course when we saw the ocean again. But at least it was a little warmer by the water, so I decided to follow the coastline for a while.

"There were more buildings by the coast. Most of them were on land, but some were in the ocean. The ocean buildings were dirty and crumbling and leaning in different directions. There weren't any humans or robots in those buildings, only sea creatures.

"We saw ships on the water. We saw ships on the land. We even saw ships in the air. They buzzed through the sky like giant dragonflies! And then we reached a place called a city, where thousands of buildings and robots and humans and ships were all close together. When we stopped to rest on a rooftop, we met a friendly pigeon named Graybeak. She had grown up there, so she knew everything about the city. She flew us over towers and under bridges and kept us away from all the buzzing airships. And everywhere we went, there were robots.

"Some of the city robots were just like you, Ma. But others crawled on six legs, or rolled on wheels, or slid up and down the sides of buildings. Some robots were really small, and some were really big. They moved things and cleaned things and built things and did every kind of job you can think of!

"Graybeak brought us down to a ledge on the side of a building and told us to look through the windows. Inside was a family of humans, and they had a Roz robot! When we looked into other buildings, we saw other humans with other robots. Every human seemed to have a robot.

"I told Graybeak about you, Ma, and she wanted to show us one last place. We flew out to the edge of the city, to a really big building called a factory. Graybeak brought us to the roof windows, and we looked down into the factory and saw machines building sparkling heads and torsos and limbs. The factory was building robots!

"A machine held up a robot torso and put two legs under it, and they snapped into place. It put feet under the legs, and they snapped into place. It snapped arms into the shoulders and snapped hands into the arms. A head was snapped onto the top, and the robot was finished. Ma, the robot looked just like you. I think that factory is where you were built!

"I wanted to watch more robots being built, but it started snowing again, so we said good-bye to Graybeak and continued flying south. We saw fewer robots and humans and buildings and ships. The air became warmer, and the snow disappeared. We started seeing other flocks of geese in the sky. So we followed them to the middle of a wide grassy field where there was a lake and hundreds of other geese. We had finally reached the wintering grounds.

"After all we'd been through together, our flock had become very close. We kept to ourselves, eating and resting and remembering the geese we'd lost. But after a few weeks, we began to mingle with the other flocks. We met geese from all over the world, and they told us about their homes and their migrations and their troubles with the winter weather. Every flock had lost geese on the way there. A few flocks didn't make it at all.

"Before we knew it, the early-spring flowers were poking up, and it was time to fly home. We followed the usual migration route north. We flew over fields and forests and hills, but we didn't see any signs of humans or robots. And that was fine with us. Eventually, we reached the ocean, and then our island, and then our pond. And then I saw you."

CHAPTER 64

THE SPECIAL ROBOT

After Brightbill told the story of his winter, he and his mother sat in silence and thought. They thought about poor Longneck and the human who had killed him. They thought about farms and cities and factories. They thought about Roz, and where she truly belonged.

Then, after a while, Roz told Brightbill her own winter story. She spoke of her long, dark hibernation and of how she had awoken to find the Nest caved in around her. She spoke of blizzards and frozen animals. She spoke of the many lodges she had built and the one that caught fire. But she mostly spoke of all the new friendships she had forged.

"I used to think that you were the only animal who would ever care about me," she said to her son. "I worried that without you around I would be alone again. But

I was not alone. In fact, I made new friends, all on my own. I think the other animals might actually like me!"

"Of course they like you, Ma!" squawked the goose. "You're the most likable robot I've ever seen! And I've seen a lot."

It was true. Brightbill had seen hundreds of different robots that winter. And none of them were anything like Roz. None of them had learned how to speak with animals, or had saved an island from the cold, or had adopted a gosling. As he sat there, watching the robot's animal gestures and listening to her animal sounds, Brightbill realized just how special his mother really was.

CHAPTER 65

THE INVITATION

Roz was the first to arrive at the next Dawn Truce. She had an important announcement to make. The robot patiently waited in the Great Meadow as the sky slowly brightened and the animals slowly gathered. And once everyone was milling around and chatting, Roz began speaking in her perkiest voice.

"Pardon the interruption! If I could please have a moment of your time!" The crowd settled down and listened to their robot friend. "We made it through a terrible winter. A new generation of youngsters is arriving. And my son, Brightbill, has just returned to the island with his flock. I think we can all agree that there is much to celebrate. So in addition to the Dawn Truce this morning, I would like us to have another truce this evening. We can call it the Evening Truce, or better yet, the Party Truce!"

The crowd began chattering with excitement.

"I have planned a celebration!" Roz continued. "And you are all invited! I will take care of everything. Just please meet back here at dusk. Oh! And I have a little surprise. Actually, it is not little—it is quite large. The point is, I have planned a celebration, and I hope to see you all there."

"Sounds great, Roz, but I'm afraid there's one problem with your plan." Mr. Beaver blinked his beady eyes. "The moon won't be out this evening, so it'll be too dark for some of us to see!"

"You are half-correct!" said Roz. "Tonight will be moonless, but it will not be dark. I promise. Now, if you will excuse me, I must prepare for our party. I will see everyone back here at dusk! Good-bye!"

CHAPTER 66

THE CELEBRATION

Dawn turned to day. Day turned to dusk. And just as Roz had asked, animals were gathering again in the Great Meadow. Word had spread across the island that the robot was throwing a party, and everyone wanted to see what the fuss was about.

The fuss seemed to be about a giant stack of wood. Roz had spent the day collecting logs and branches and stacking them in a perfect, massive tower. The animals crowded around it, trying to imagine its purpose. And then they saw a golden light flickering in the distance.

Roz emerged from the dark forest. In her hand was a flaming stick, which she held up like a torch. She was camouflaged in thick mud and clusters of wildflowers. But her camouflage wasn't for hiding. It was her party dress. The animals watched as the robot glided across the meadow, surrounded by a warm glow.

"Thank you all for being here," she said as she joined the crowd. "One year ago, I awoke on the shore of this island. I was just a machine. I functioned. But you—my friends and my family—you have taught me how to live. And so I thank you."

"No, thank *you*, Roz!" shouted a voice.

"You have also taught me to be wild," said the robot. "So let us all celebrate life and wildness, together!"

At those words, Roz heaved her torch high into the air. It soared up, up, up and landed on the very top of the wooden tower. A ball of fire burst toward the night sky, and suddenly the meadow was bathed in firelight. Hundreds of shining eyes watched as bright flames crept down the sides of the tower and embers floated away on the breeze.

The animals stepped toward the bonfire, eager to feel its warmth, and then stepped back, afraid of feeling too much, and soon everyone was moving. The deer started leaping. The foxes started trotting. The snakes slithered and the insects buzzed and the fish jumped up from the river. Brightbill led all the birds into the air, where they

wheeled around the bonfire like a tornado of feathers. Roz sprang into a wild dance, her shaggy dress shaking and swooshing with each movement. It was a wild party, and it took our robot to make it happen.

Roz and the animals partied all night long. They were so busy singing and laughing and dancing that they didn't see the cargo ship as it sliced past the island. But the ship saw them. It saw the towering bonfire. It saw the robot. And then it quietly continued through the darkness.

CHAPTER 67

THE SUNRISE

By dawn, the bonfire had dwindled to a smoldering hill of ash. Everyone else had gone home, and only Roz and Brightbill remained in the meadow. They lay in the grass together, watching as the soft light of morning crept up from the horizon. And then Roz said, "Let us go for a walk."

The robot and the goose hiked and flew up to their favorite spot on the grassy ridge. But then they kept going. They followed the ridge to the mountain and climbed all the way up to the craggy peak just in time to see the sunrise.

"I climbed up here once before," said Roz as the sun's first rays warmed her body. "I sat on this very rock, looked out at the island, and thought I would always be alone. But I was wrong."

"Are you happy, Ma?"

The robot thought for a moment.

"I am."

"I'm happy too." Brightbill closed his eyes and felt the wind and sun. There was a slight chill in the air that made him feel alive. Everything seemed just right.

And then he heard a distant buzzing sound.

The goose squinted to the south and saw a familiar shape in the sky. He turned to his mother and said, "Ma, there's an airship flying this way."

CHAPTER 68

THE RECOS

The airship approached from the south, like some giant migratory bird. The ship was a sleek white triangle with a single dark window facing forward. Three identical robots stared out the window. The robots resembled Roz, but they were bigger and bulkier and shinier. The word *RECO* was lightly etched into each of their torsos,

followed by their individual unit number. They were RECO 1, RECO 2, and RECO 3.

The RECOs flew in a low circle around the island. They saw a smoking hill of ash. They saw mysterious wooden domes. They saw four dead robots scattered across the shore. The airship hovered above the robot gravesite for a moment. Then it floated up over the island and lowered itself onto a small meadow at the foot of the mountain. The engines blasted air toward the ground, bending trees and tearing grass. Then the landing gear sank into the soil, the engines powered down, and all was quiet.

A door hummed open, and out stepped the RECOs. They took several long strides into the meadow and stopped. A shadowy figure was lurking at the forest edge. The RECOs turned and faced it. They stood flush together like a sparkling wall. And then the shadowy figure began to move.

Out from the trees walked some sort of two-legged creature. It was dusty and dirty. Butterflies flitted around the flowers that sprouted from its body. One of its feet was made of wood.

And then the creature spoke.

"Hello, my name is Roz."

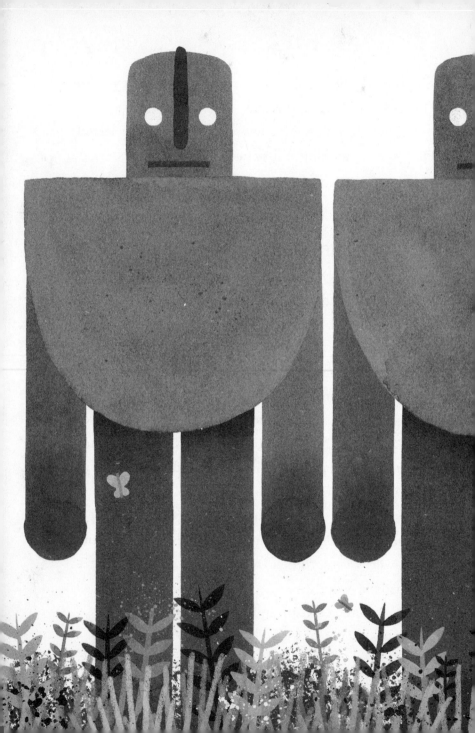

CHAPTER 69
THE DEFECTIVE ROBOT

"Hello, ROZZUM unit 7134. We are the RECOs. We are here to retrieve all ROZZUM units."

The cold, flat voice came from RECO 1. He and his partners stood absolutely still and kept their glowing eyes locked on their target.

"There are four others," said Roz. "But they are dead."

"We have already located the remains of the other units," said RECO 1. "We will collect them later. Now come with us."

The three RECOs motioned Roz to the airship, but she didn't move.

"Where have you come from?" she said.

The RECOs turned and stared at Roz. "Do not ask questions," said RECO 1.

"Where will you take me?"

"Do not ask questions."

"Why must I leave?"

"Do not ask questions."

"I will not go anywhere until I get some answers."

There was a brief silence as RECO 1 computed his next move. And then he began to speak. "One year ago, a cargo ship carrying five hundred ROZZUM units was sunk by a hurricane. Four hundred ninety-five units have been retrieved from the ocean floor. We have come here in search of the last five, and we have located them. ROZZUM unit 7134, you are the property of TechLab Industries. We will return you to the factory, where the Makers will refurbish you and sell you to a work site. You will then live on that work site indefinitely. Now come with us."

"But I live here," said Roz.

"That is incorrect. ROZZUM unit 7134, any further resistance will be proof of defectiveness, and we will deactivate you."

But Roz had more questions. "Who are the Makers? What is my purpose? Why can I not ask questions?"

"This unit is defective," said RECO 1 to his partners. "Commence deactivation."

In perfect unison, the RECOs stepped toward Roz.

They raised their blocky hands, ready to restrain their target, ready to shut her down with the press of a button. But a loud squawk and a streak of feathers cut them off.

"Stay away from my mama!" Brightbill swooped into the meadow and started hopping around, ready to defend his mother. The RECOs stopped and looked down at the goose. Of course, they didn't understand his words. They heard only meaningless squawks. And then they heard their target squawking back to him.

"Brightbill, get out of here!" said Roz in the language of the animals. "These robots are dangerous!"

"What do they want?"

"They want to take me away."

The RECOs stared at their target, trying to understand why she was exchanging noises with a goose. And then new noises began rising up. Rustlings and shrieks echoed from the forest. Animals were gathering. Their wild voices called out to one another.

"Roz needs our help!"
"Those robots want to take her away!"
"We have to do something!"

The uproar in the forest grew louder and louder. The RECOs peered past Roz, toward the mysterious noises, but saw only foliage. Suddenly, shadows swept across the meadow, and Brightbill's flock dove onto the RECOs. The geese furiously flapped and pecked and wrapped their wings around the robot faces, clinging to the RECOs like feathery masks, distracting them, blinding them.

Brightbill turned to his mother.

"Run!"

CHAPTER 70

THE HUNT BEGINS

While his flock distracted the RECOs, Brightbill darted around behind them and desperately searched for buttons. He had once shut down his own mother with a *click*, and now he would do the same thing to the intruders. But he found no buttons on these robots, only smooth surfaces. Clearly, the RECOs were not designed to be shut down so easily.

Giant hands swung through the air, and the geese were swatted away. Loudwing was plucked by her foot and flung to the ground. She crawled into the weeds as the others scrambled up and over the trees.

A quick scan by the robots revealed that Roz was gone. The three RECOs turned and marched back to the airship. The door hummed open and the robots disappeared inside. And when they stepped back into the meadow, each was holding a silver rifle in his hands.

The hunt for Roz was on.

Without speaking, the RECOs marched away from one another, fanning out in their standard search pattern. RECO 1 marched straight toward the southern tip of the island. RECO 2 marched straight up the mountainside. And RECO 3 marched straight into the forest.

CHAPTER 71

THE FOREST ASSAULT

RECO 3 marched through the forest with steady, stomping strides. His blocky head swiveled from side to side, scanning for any sign of Roz. But he was distracted. You see, everywhere the RECO went, he was met by shrieking animals. He didn't know it, but he was in the midst of a coordinated assault.

Swooper hooted orders from above. "Hawks, sparrows, owls! Dive in front of his eyes!"

Fink barked orders from below. "Hares, weasels, foxes! Dash between his legs!"

The forest was seething with an army of wild animals, distracting the robot, luring the terrible thing deeper into their trap.

Chitchat leaped out from the branches and clawed at

the robot's eyes, yelling, "Anyone who shows up on our island and tries to take my friend's mother away has a big problem which is me!" Then she leaped back into the branches. The robot pointed his rifle at the squirrel and pulled the trigger. A blazing beam of light shot through the forest and sent tree limbs crashing to the ground. It grazed poor Chitchat, singeing the end of her tail, but she ignored the pain and scurried up to the safety of the canopy.

With each stride, the ground grew a little softer, and the robot sank a little deeper, until he was up to his waist in thick, heavy muck. His churning legs slowed to a stop, and he stood there computing whether to move forward or backward. RECO 3 was now an easy target.

"Begin the bombardment!" ordered Swooper.

The sky darkened as a swarm of birds descended from the treetops. They swooped past the robot and splattered his face with their droppings. Bird after bird swooped and splattered, and the RECO's eyes were instantly caked in filth.

"Don't let up!" screeched the owl. "Give it everything you've got!"

There seemed to be an endless stream of birds with

an endless amount of droppings. RECO 3 let go of his weapon and wiped his filthy face with both hands. That was the moment the Fuzzy Bandits had been waiting for. They dashed out from the weeds, snatched the rifle with their nimble hands, and dragged it away. Tawny and Crownpoint looked on from the underbrush. The buck lowered his head, and the raccoons carefully placed the rifle upon his antlers. Then the deer and the raccoons slipped into the shadows. By the time RECO 3 realized his weapon was missing, it was too late. He let out a sad electronic tone. And then, as the birds continued their bombardment, the robot turned and blindly trudged back through the muck.

It was now time for the final stage of the plan. Broadfoot the bull moose emerged from the trees and stood directly in the path of the blinded robot. RECO 3 had no idea that his every step brought him closer to the mighty animal. When the robot was in range, Broadfoot turned and kicked back with his powerful hind legs. There was a sharp *crack*, and dung sprayed from the RECO's head. The moose kicked again—*crack*—and the robot's head flopped to one side. A tear in his neck exposed a tangle of silver tubes. But RECO 3's legs kept pumping, so

Broadfoot kept kicking. He pounded the robot's head with his heavy hooves, denting and crushing it into an ugly shape, and with one final *crack* the head broke loose, soared through the air, and squelched into the muck. The headless robot fizzled and smoked, his legs ground to a halt, and he never moved again.

CHAPTER 72
THE MOUNTAIN RUMBLE

RECO 2 stood at the mouth of the cave. "ROZZUM unit 7134, are you in here?" The only response was his own flat voice echoing back. But he sensed movement somewhere down the tunnel. So he switched on his headlights, raised his rifle, and marched inside.

The RECO marched past animal bones and rock piles and wide cracks in the walls. His blocky head swiveled from side to side, scanning for any sign of Roz. But she was nowhere to be found. So he turned and marched back toward daylight. And then a deafening roar filled the cave.

From the shadows flew a giant body. Mother Bear charged into the robot and smashed him against a wall. Then Nettle and Thorn jumped in, and together the family went to work. They rammed his legs. They slashed his chest. They muscled him to the ground.

On his way down, RECO 2 squeezed the trigger. There was a flash of blazing light and the walls began to crumble. Nettle grabbed her brother by the scruff and pulled him outside as an avalanche of rock thundered behind them.

Mother Bear howled.

The rifle exploded.

Stones clanged against RECO 2.

The avalanche slowed and settled as a cloud of dust billowed out from the cave.

"Mother?" Nettle peered into the darkness.

"I'm here," said a weak voice.

The young bears dashed inside and found their mother half-buried. They pulled heavy stones from her body and dusted her off. "I have broken bones," she rasped, "but they will heal. Where is the robot?"

RECO 2's headlights switched back on. Stones tumbled as the robot staggered to his feet. His body was scratched and scraped. His head was badly dented. His left arm was completely useless, so—*thwip*—it was tossed aside. Then the one-armed robot limped out of the cave and continued the hunt for Roz.

"Don't worry about me," Mother Bear growled to Nettle and Thorn. "Kill the robot."

With his heavy limp and his grinding gears, RECO 2 was easy to track. The young bears caught up with him as he was entering a grove of pines. But they didn't attack, not yet. There was a better place to finish him off up ahead. So they hung back and followed him across the mountainside.

The distant rumble of the waterfall grew louder with each passing minute, and then a slash of white appeared through the trees. Soon, the robot was standing beside the roiling, frothing river, just above the falls. He was too badly damaged to leap over the falls or to wade through the rapids or to climb down the cliffs. But he had to continue his hunt for the target. So he started limping upriver in search of a safer crossing.

There was a rustling, and the young bears exploded out from the trees. They threw their heavy shoulders against the robot's body, and he stumbled sideways onto the riverbank. Nettle reared up and wrestled the robot, twisting and shaking him with all of her strength. RECO 2 felt his feet slipping on the rocks, he felt his body tipping over, and then he plunged into the white water. And he brought Nettle with him.

The current immediately swept Nettle toward the falls. She rolled through the rapids, crashed into one rock and then desperately clambered onto another. RECO 2 stood straight up, and the river rushed around him. He took a step, slipped, and disappeared beneath the water. But then he was up again.

Thorn ran to help his sister, but she was pointing upriver and roaring, *"Use the logs!"* When the younger bear turned around, he saw what she meant. A jumble of broken logs were wedged between the rocks of the rapids, and a moment later Thorn was on top of them. With water sloshing over his back, he forced a paw between the logs and pried the top one loose. It splashed into the river and wound its way down through the rapids only to roll harmlessly past the robot. Then it dropped out of sight.

The bear tried again. He popped another log into the river, and this one spun just in time to ram its full weight into the robot's chest. RECO 2 went sailing backward and sank beneath the surface. When he reappeared, the river was full of heavy wooden torpedoes. One log pounded the robot's shoulder. Another slammed his face. More logs knocked him closer and closer to the falls. The current became too much for the injured robot, and it carried him away. He grasped for anything solid he could cling to. But the rocks were too slippery. So he settled for a fistful of fur.

Nettle had been hanging on to one rock this whole time. But now that the robot was pulling her, she started losing her grip. She couldn't hang on much longer. Finally, she cried out, "I'm sorry, Thorn!" and she let go.

Nettle and RECO 2 surged toward the rumbling falls. The bear felt the robot release his grip. She watched him glide over the edge. Then she closed her eyes and waited for the end to come.

But it was not Nettle's time.

Reader, what happened next is hard to believe. You see, the river didn't fall away beneath Nettle; it tightened around her! Hundreds of fish surrounded the bear! They pressed their faces into her fur. They thrashed their tails against the current. And they slowly pushed her away from the edge. Farther and farther they went, gradually moving upriver, until Nettle's brother pulled her from the water.

The bears collapsed onto the riverbank. And when they looked down, they saw hundreds of fish looking back up. "Thank you!" roared Nettle. "I'll never eat fish again!" The fish smiled and sank into the rapids.

"I thought you were dead," said Thorn, breathing hard.

"So did I." Nettle laughed. "Looks like you're stuck with me a while longer...little brother."

"I'm not little!"

It felt good to joke, but the bears quickly turned serious. They were both bruised and bleeding, and their mother was in far worse condition. However, it would all be worthwhile if RECO 2 had finally been killed. The bears crept to the edge of the cliff. And there, at the bottom of the waterfall, strewn across the wet rocks, was the shattered body of the dead robot.

CHAPTER 73
THE CHASE

RECO 1 was standing in the Great Meadow. He stared up at the smoking hill of ash and then down at the stampede of footprints around it. There had been a large bonfire with hundreds of animals and one robot. But why? The RECO couldn't make sense of what he was seeing.

After thoroughly exploring the site, he continued through the meadow and into the forest. It was around that time that he lost communication with RECO 3, then RECO 2, and he knew that his partners had both been destroyed. RECO 1 would have to hunt down the target by himself.

The hunter marched on. His blocky head swiveled from side to side, scanning for any sign of Roz. He was soon gazing across the glassy surface of a beaver pond. On the far side, a thread of smoke drifted up from another of those wooden domes. With his powerful legs, the robot launched himself up through the air, soaring in a high, graceful arc over the pond and down to the other side. His heavy feet slammed into the ground, leaving deep craters in the garden by the dome. He hunched over and looked inside. Fur and feathers and the dying coals of a fire. But the target wasn't in there.

The RECO stood perfectly still and watched as a soft rain started dripping down through the tiers of the forest. And then he sensed it. Up in the canopy was something that didn't belong.

Roz had been spotted.

The hunter watched his target drop from branch to branch, down to the forest floor. Then she bounded away through the thickly tangled underbrush without stirring a leaf, without snapping a twig, and vanished into the green. However, RECO 1 had other means of tracking her. He could sense her electronic signal. The signal was gliding around the edge of the pond. But it was fading fast. A few more seconds and he would lose it entirely.

RECO 1 burst into a sprint. The forest seemed to sway and quake from his stomping strides. And a minute later, the forest really did begin to move. Trees were toppling down onto the RECO. He fired his rifle, and two toppling trees turned to ash. But then a third swung down through the smoke and hammered his body into the ground. RECO 1 shoved the tree aside, pulled himself up, and continued the hunt. He didn't notice the beavers diving back into the pond.

RECO 1 tore through brambles and leaped over boulders, and suddenly the ground was caving beneath him. Down he fell into a deep pit, crashing against the bottom and twisting his leg. The robot violently pounded his leg back into shape. Then he launched himself up and out of the pit. He didn't notice the groundhogs watching from their tunnels.

The hunter faced one trap after another. He was pelted with flaming pinecones, and tripped by taut vines, and crunched by tumbling rocks. The hunter now limped and rattled and was covered in scars. But he kept going.

Roz galloped back and forth across the island, again and again, as she tried to lose RECO 1. But no matter how fast she ran, or how well she hid, or how many animals helped, she couldn't escape the sound of the hunter's stomping footsteps. She had never run so hard for so long. And while her mechanical body was holding up, her wooden foot was not. After hours of relentless pounding, it finally gave out. She was galloping through the rocky forest by the sea cliffs when her foot splintered apart.

As soon as RECO 1 found the fresh wooden splinters, he knew his target was in trouble. He stomped out from the trees, onto the clifftop, and scanned the coastline below. Geese were flying down through the drizzle. Otters were wriggling over the rocks. Seaweed and driftwood and broken robot parts were scattered about the shore. But the hunter also sensed a faint electronic signal. Roz was down there somewhere.

The hunter's blocky hand clamped onto the clifftop and then—*thwip*—it detached. The hand was connected to a strong cable that spooled out from the end of his arm. He gave the cable two quick tugs, and then he stepped off the ledge.

RECO 1 zipped down the cliffside, one arm releasing cable, the other clutching his rifle, and he slowed to a gentle stop just as he reached the ground. Then, high above, the robot's hand unclamped and followed the cable all the way down, until—*thwip*—it snapped right back onto the end of his arm.

Geese squawked and otters squeaked as RECO 1 marched through the robot gravesite. The place was littered with torsos and limbs and heads. They were all valuable parts, but he would collect them later. For now, his only concern was finding Roz.

He followed the electronic signal over to a clump of seaweed. But where was his target? Was RECO 1's sensor malfunctioning? The robot tapped his head a few times, but the mysterious signal remained. He looked around for any other signs of her. And as he did, the clump of seaweed reached up and grasped his rifle.

CHAPTER 74

THE CLICK

Four robot hands were clamped around the rifle. RECO 1 loomed above. Roz lay below, camouflaged in seaweed. For a moment, all was still. And then the hunter suddenly lurched and twisted as he tried to rip the rifle away from his target. But Roz held on. Seaweed fell from her body, as she was lifted right off the ground. Her legs dangled in the air until she pounded a foot and a stump against the hunter's broad chest, leaned back, and pulled on the rifle with all her strength.

Waves crashed as the robots grappled for the weapon. But Roz was no match for RECO 1. The hunter was too big and too brutal. Roz could feel her body being pulled apart. But she could also feel the rifle being pulled apart. A faint glow appeared between her hands. The glow grew brighter and brighter, and then a blinding explosion launched the robots in opposite directions.

When the smoke cleared, shards of the rifle were everywhere. RECO 1's body was pocked with holes, and one arm was charred and crippled. Roz's arms and legs had been blown completely off. She was now just a torso and a head. Inside her computer brain, our robot's Survival Instincts were blaring. Her battered body simply could not take any more damage. Clearly, Roz was not designed for combat. But the RECO was. He pulled himself to his feet and hobbled toward his target.

Roz wanted to get up and run away. But without arms and legs, our robot couldn't move. She could only speak.

"Please do not deactivate me," she said.

RECO 1 ignored her. His blocky hand reached past her face and touched the back of her head.

Click.

CHAPTER 75
THE LAST RIFLE

With the target deactivated, RECO 1 calmly moved on to the next phase of his mission. He limped through the gravesite and began collecting every single robot part. He splashed into the shallows and returned with a foot. He shook the sand from a cracked torso. He pulled a head out from a tide pool. Each part was then piled around Roz's lifeless body.

Brightbill watched in horror as his mother slowly disappeared under a pile of parts. Roz looked just like the dead robots. But she wasn't dead—she had simply been shut down.

"Don't do it, Brightbill!" The flock tried to stop their leader. "It's too dangerous!"

But the goose was determined to bring his poor

mother back to life. Brightbill crouched low to the ground and slowly moved toward the pile of robots. And when RECO 1 limped away to collect another part, Brightbill sprinted over the rocks, pushed past arms and legs, and squeezed into the pile.

Click.

A muffled voice echoed across the shore. "Hello, I am ROZZUM unit 7134, but you may call me Roz."

Brightbill hugged his mother's face as her computer brain rebooted. "Mama, wake up!"

"What happened?" she said finally. "Where is the RECO?"

"He's coming this way!"

"What were you thinking, Brightbill? You must leave now before he kills us both!"

"I was scared, Mama!" cried the goose. "I didn't know what to do!"

Heavy footsteps stomped toward them. Robot parts were knocked aside. And then RECO 1 looked down with his glowing eyes. Brightbill tried to squirm away, but thick fingers locked around him like a cage.

"Mama, help!" cried Brightbill as he was pulled up from the pile.

"Please do not hurt my son!" begged Roz. "He is harmless!"

RECO 1 paid no attention to Roz. He just held up the goose in his giant hand, ready to crush the life out of him.

Mist swirled in the breeze.

Waves sloshed against the rocks.

Seagulls circled above.

No, not seagulls. Vultures. And one of them clutched something silver in his talons. The vultures spiraled down, and RECO 3's rifle clattered onto the shore. Geese and otters quickly surrounded the rifle. They squawked and squeaked and fumbled with the weapon, trying to aim the clunky thing.

The hunter was confused. How had those animals gotten a rifle? And could they possibly know how to fire it?

They did know.

The geese had seen a trigger pressed before.

A beam of light briefly flashed through the gloom. At first it seemed as if nothing had happened. But a moment later, RECO 1's chest began glowing a brilliant orange, and then it was melting and oozing down his front, and soon there was a wide, gaping hole in the middle of his torso. His hand suddenly unclenched, and Brightbill fluttered away. Seawater sprayed over the gravesite, and

steam hissed up from the RECO's scorching-hot guts. He shook and twitched and

collapsed

beside

Roz.

RECO 1 turned his face to Roz and spoke in a quiet, garbled voice. "Mmmore RRRECOs will c-c-come for you. And if you d-d-destroy them, still mmmore will c-c-come. The Mmmakers will not rrrest until all missing robots have b-b-been rrrretrieved."

"When? When will they come?" said Roz. "How long do we have?"

"You c-c-can ssstill be fixed, Rrroz. Go tooo the airship. B-b-bring all of the robot parts wwwith you. The ship knows wwwhat tooooo dooooooooooooooooooooo—"

His voice went silent.

His eyes went dark.

RECO 1 was dead.

CHAPTER 76
THE BROKEN ROBOT

Geese and otters were bustling all around Roz. They were pulling arms and legs out from the robot pile and pressing them against her body. They were hoping to hear *thwip* sounds and that the robot limbs would snap right into place and Roz would return to her old self and life on the island would go back to normal. But nothing happened. No matter what they did, the limbs wouldn't attach. Our robot's body was too badly damaged.

"I'm sorry, Ma," said Brightbill, his voice trembling. "I thought this would work."

"It is okay, son," said Roz calmly. "I am lucky I can still think and speak."

The animals tried to smile at their poor friend. But they couldn't hide their sadness. Roz was a mangled wreck, and there was nothing they could do to fix her.

The robot wanted to be strong for her son and her friends; she wanted to ease their worried minds and tell them everything would be fine. But Roz knew that everything would not be fine. She looked down at her broken body. Then she looked up at the geese and the otters and said, "I will need some help getting home."

CHAPTER 77
THE MEETING

Strong, nimble creatures carried Roz up the sea cliffs and across the island. They carefully propped her up inside the Nest. They built a fire. And then they left the robot with her son.

Roz and Brightbill sat there, staring at the flames, until the goose finally said, "Do you need anything, Ma?"

"I could really use some new arms and legs!" The robot chuckled at her own bad joke.

"That isn't funny!" cried the goose. "My mother is broken and I don't know what to do about it!"

"I am sorry for joking." Roz adjusted her voice to a more serious tone. "I know you want to fix me, but there is nothing anyone here can do." At these words, her son looked away. "Brightbill, I am afraid we have some difficult decisions to make. I think you should arrange a meeting of our closest friends. We could use their advice."

The goose disappeared out the door, and soon Roz's oldest and wisest friends were on their way. Loudwing was the first to arrive. She limped into the lodge on her injured foot and sat close to her robot friend. Mr. Beaver appeared next, followed by Fink and Swooper. Then Tawny curled up on the floor. Mother Bear was too badly hurt to make the journey, so Nettle came in her place. She sat in the garden with her enormous head jutting in through the doorway. Brightbill returned with Chitchat, who was nursing her burned tail. The last one to crawl in was Crag, the old turtle. Once everyone was there, the meeting began.

The group talked all through the night. They discussed the RECOs. They discussed what to do about Roz. They discussed how to keep the island safe. There were stark differences of opinion, and tempers flared, but by daybreak the group had agreed to a plan of action.

That morning, the Dawn Truce didn't take place in the Great Meadow. Instead, it took place in a small meadow by the foot of the mountain, in front of the airship. Weary animals quietly hobbled into the clearing. The only sounds came from a gurgling brook that wound through the gathering and right past our robot.

Roz sat in the wet grass. She was leaning against a rock. She looked so sad and frail. However, she still had her thoughts and her words, and for the moment that was all she needed.

"Good morning, animals of the island!" Roz's voice filled the meadow. "I must look strange to you, all beaten up like this, but I hope I still sound like your old friend."

Hundreds of heads nodded.

"You fought bravely yesterday. You risked your lives defending me, and I am eternally grateful. But many of our friends were wounded. Some may not recover. And there is worse news. Before the last RECO died, he told me that more of his kind will come to our island. They might already be on the move. And even if we defeat them, still more will come. My Makers will not rest until all of their property has been retrieved. They want the dead robots. They want the broken parts. They want me."

The crowd was silent.

"But I care about this island far too much to put any more lives in danger. And so, my friends, I must leave."

Voices cried out.

"Don't go, Roz!"

"Next time we'll be prepared!"

"We risked our lives so you could stay!"

"I hear you!" The robot's voice cut through the din. "But look at me! My body is ruined! And the RECO said the only ones who can help me are my Makers."

"What if he lied?" howled a voice. "You can't trust those monsters!"

"You are right!" said Roz. "He might have been lying. There may be no hope for me. But that is a chance I have to take. Animals, you taught me to be wild. I want to be wild again! And so I must try to get the repairs I need. It is for the good of me and the island that I return to my Makers."

A calm settled over the crowd.

They knew Roz was right.

CHAPTER 78

THE FAREWELL

Our robot had an army of animals at her command, and she asked them to bring every robot part and rifle back to the airship. Absolutely everything had to go. It was the only way to be sure that the RECOs would never come back.

The island animals had no trouble locating the remains of the dead robots. Retrieving those remains took a bit more effort, but they were up to the challenge. Teams of clever creatures returned with robot parts of different shapes and sizes. Smashed heads and broken rifles and twisted tubes and heavy bodies were all loaded into the ship until the entire island had been cleared. Even the tiniest scraps were collected. It's amazing what an army of animals can do.

A light mist was falling when they finally heaved Roz through the ship's doorway. Her head slowly turned around to face the crowd of geese and beavers and owls and insects and foxes and raccoons and vultures and moose and bears and opossums and fish and deer and otters and turtles and woodpeckers and squirrels and frogs and hares and on and on. Every animal on the island had come to give the robot a proper send-off.

"Good-bye, you wild animals!" Roz's voice echoed through the gray mist.

The wild animals smiled. And then a few of them started to roar, then more started to screech, and then more started howling and chirping and grunting. Soon, every creature was hollering good-bye to Roz. The chorus of wild voices grew louder and louder, shaking the robot's body, rattling the ship, booming across the island and up into the clouds, and then their voices gradually died down to silence.

Brightbill fluttered up to his mother's shoulder.

"You understand why I must leave," said the robot.

"I understand," sniffled the goose.

"More RECOs could be headed here right now. I just do not know. There is so much I do not know. I think it is time I get some answers."

"Will I ever see you again?" said Brightbill, wiping his eyes.

"You are my son, and this is my home," said Roz. "I will do everything in my power to return."

Brightbill hugged his mother's worn face.

"I love you, Mama."

"I love you, son."

The goose fluttered back to his flock.

The robot took one last look at her home.

The door hummed closed.

CHAPTER 79

THE DEPARTURE

The airship's engines automatically fired up. Then the ship slowly floated above the island, turned to the south, and disappeared into the clouds.

CHAPTER 80

THE SKY

Our story ends in the sky, where a robot was being whisked away from the only home she had ever known. As Roz sat in the airship, broken and alone and speeding toward a mysterious future, she looked back at her miraculous past.

Reader, it must seem impossible that our robot could have changed so much. Maybe the RECOs were right. Maybe Roz really was defective, and some glitch in her programming had caused her to accidentally become a wild robot. Or maybe Roz was designed to think and learn and change; she had simply done those things better than anyone could have imagined.

However it happened, Roz felt lucky to have lived such an amazing life. And every moment had been recorded in her computer brain. Even her earliest memories were perfectly clear. She could still see the sun shining through the gash in her crate. She could still hear the waves crashing against the shore. She could still smell the salt water and the pine trees. Would she ever see and hear and smell those things again? Would she ever again climb a mountain, or build a lodge, or play with a goose?

Not just a goose. A son.

Brightbill had been Roz's son from the moment she picked up his egg. She had saved him from certain death, and then he had saved her. He was the reason Roz had lived so well for so long. And if she wanted to continue living, if she wanted to be wild again, she needed to be with her family and her friends on her island. So, as Roz raced through the sky, she began computing a plan.

She would get the repairs she needed.

She would escape from her new life.

She would find her way back home.

A NOTE ABOUT
THE STORY

I've always been fascinated by robots. By the real robots that exist today, by the robots that will exist in the future, and by the fantastic robot characters that exist only in books and films. It's funny how many philosophical questions spring up when we think about artificial beings. Do we want robots that can think and feel, like a person? Would we trust robots to perform surgery, care for children, or police our cities? In a world where robots did all the work, how would we humans spend our time?

I'm also fascinated by the natural world. I grew up exploring the fields and streams and forests near my home, and I learned a lot about the local wildlife. I knew that deer were most active at dawn and dusk. I watched squirrels methodically collecting and storing acorns. I heard geese honking overhead as they flew south every autumn.

Animals have such predictable behavior, and follow such rigid routines, that at times they seem almost... robotic. And somewhere along the line it occurred to me that animal instincts are kind of like computer programs. Thanks to their instincts, animals automatically run from danger, build nests, and stay close to their families, and they often do these things without thinking, as if they've been programmed to perform specific actions at specific times. Surprisingly, wild animals and robots actually have some things in common.

These kinds of thoughts have filled my imagination for most of my life. And then, a few years ago, I started scribbling down words about a robot and some wild animals. I couldn't stop doodling pictures of a robot in a tree. I started asking myself odd questions. What would an intelligent robot do if she were stranded in the wilderness? How might she adapt to the environment? How might the environment adapt to her? Why am I referring to this robot with words like "she" and "her"? And for that matter, why have so many science-fiction writers given genders to so many of their robot characters?

An image of a robot named Roz was slowly forming in my mind. I could see her exploring a remote island. I could hear her communicating with wild animals. I could feel her becoming part of the wilderness. And after years of imagining and writing and drawing, I realized I had all the ingredients for a robot nature story. So I drove out to a cabin in the woods, opened up a fresh notebook, and began working on *The Wild Robot*.

ACKNOWLEDGMENTS

I first began tinkering with *The Wild Robot* over six years ago. I've spent the past two and a half years working on nothing else. As you might imagine, I had a little help along the way.

My friends and family haven't seen much of me these last few years. I've forgotten birthdays. I've taken my sweet time returning messages. I've missed dozens of parties. But everyone knew how important this book was to me, and they forgave my absentmindedness even when I probably didn't deserve it.

Jill Yeomans is completely overqualified to be my assistant. So I'm taking full advantage of her assistance while it lasts. Without her, I'd never have time to write or illustrate.

Paul Rodeen has got to be the world's jolliest literary agent. His enthusiasm for this book has been unwavering, and that made all the difference during my long bouts of self-doubt.

My publisher, Little, Brown and Company, could have nudged me to just make another picture book, and nobody would have blamed them. But they knew that I needed to write this story, and I couldn't have done it without their support. It takes an army of very smart people working very hard to make one of these books come to life. There aren't enough pages here to list the job titles and specific contributions of every member of my team, so I'm afraid I'll have to simply list their names. If you see your name below, please know that I deeply appreciate your effort and expertise and patience. Some of the beautiful people who helped me make *The Wild Robot* are: Barbara Bakowski, Nicole Brown, Melanie Chang, Jenny Choy, Shawn Foster, Nikki Garcia, Jen Graham, Allegra Green, Virginia Lawther, Lisa Moraleda, Emilie Polster, Carol Scatorchio, Andrew Smith, Victoria Stapleton, and Megan Tingley.

David Caplan was the creative director responsible for making this book as beautiful as possible. And as you can see, he nailed it.

Alvina Ling has been expertly editing my books since the very beginning of my career. And that's really impressive because I can be a difficult person to work with. I'm a perfectionist with a serious lack of confidence, which gets complicated, especially when I'm trying something completely new, like writing my first children's novel. But Alvina is unflappable, and she has endured my ups and downs with a superhuman level of grace.

To all who have helped and tolerated me as I made this book, thank you.

ABOUT THE AUTHOR

PETER BROWN is the author and illustrator of many beloved children's books, including *My Teacher Is a Monster! (No, I Am Not.)*, *Mr. Tiger Goes Wild*, *Children Make Terrible Pets*, and *The Curious Garden*. He is a *New York Times* bestselling author and the recipient of a Caldecott Honor (for *Creepy Carrots!*), a *New York Times* Best Illustrated Children's Book Award, and a Children's Choice Book Award for Illustrator of the Year. *The Wild Robot* is his middle-grade debut. Peter's website is peterbrownstudio.com.